FELLOWSHIP

COMPANION NOVEL TO THE FELLOWSHIP DYSTOPIA SERIES

LYNETTE M. BURROWS

ROCKET DOG PUBLISHING

This is a work of fiction. All characters, places, organizations, and events portrayed in this novel are either the product of the author's imagination or are used fictitiously.

———

ISBN: 978-1-7325822-6-2 (pbk.)

ISBN-13: 978-1-7325822-4-8 (kindle)

ISBN: 978-1-7325822-5-5 (ePub)

PROLOGUE

A Testament for Modern Times
"The New Book of Josiah"
Chapter 3, verses 1-18

1. *Now it came to pass, in the days after the Great War, that the children of the world did evil in the sight of the Lord.*
2. *And the anger of the Lord was kindled and He delivered to them the days of darkness called the Great Depression.*
3. *Thieves, drunkards, and murderers ruled the land known as America. Their leader, Franklin Delano Roosevelt, was assassinated; yet the people repented not.*
4. *In these dark days the peoples of Europe, Russia, and Asia turned from God. It came to pass that war erupted between them and the Third Reich.*
5. *The wicked fell upon each other and they dwelt in the darkness of their damnation.*
6. *Ten times ten thousand Britons were slain in*

> *the fields and in their homes. Their cities were destroyed, and their young men carried away into slavery.*

7. *The Britons called to America for ships and weapons and men. But the American people asked, "Why must our sons die over the sea in other people's battles?"*

8. *So it came to pass that the Americans closed their ears and would not hear the strife across the sea. For they were sore afraid.*

9. *Now there arose many prophets: Father Charles Coughlin, Gerald L. K. Smith, Francis Townsend, and William Ashley Sunday.*

10. *The greatest of these, born of the land called Virginia, in the Blue Ridge Mountains, was a man named Josiah Garret. A humble and pious man whose heart was troubled by the wickedness of his people.*

11. *God sent to him the angel, Gabriel. And Gabriel said unto him, "Rise up and walk the length and breadth of the land." And he did.*

12. *Josiah saw the grievous sins of the people of America and he was ashamed. He cried out, "Father, why hast thou forsaken us?"*

13. *And God spake, "This nation was conceived 'in liberty under God;' thou hast forsaken the Father."*

14. *"Woe be unto this wicked and faithless generation. In as much as ye shall repent, I will cleanse you of your iniquities.*

15. *"To him who doth not come to me with a broken heart and contrite spirit, I will blot out his name from the Book of Life."*

16. *It came to pass that Josiah made the people naked to their shame. And when the people heard him speak the words of the Lord in their synagogues, and in their temples, and in their kingdom halls, and in their churches, they fell down upon their faces and begged His forgiveness.*

17. *And the Lord blessed those who took Fellowship with Him.*

18. *And remembering His covenant with Noah, God sent not the waters but the angels, the Azrael, to cleanse the wicked from the face of the land.*

CHAPTER 1

FELLOWSHIP.

One word and Ian Hobart's world teetered into not-safe. The reporters' voices fell, the remainder of their conversation now muted by the clack and ratchet and ding of their typewriters.

Ian plastered a smile on his face and plopped back into his seat on the copyboy bench. The relentless thump and clatter heartbeat of the presses in the basement vibrated the floor, his shoes, his bones as if in warning.

The rank sweat and burnt coffee that infused the air were part of what he loved about the tiny newsroom. Sure, the work program took him out of high school for half the day. But the energy in the room, the never-ending, got-to-know-more quest, *that* sparked his soul. Until that single word cast a shroud of uncertainty.

"1860-1960, a hundred years of unbiased reporting," *The Chronicle's* slogan this year, inspired him and filled him with pride.

But unbiased—and the Fellowship—Could. Not. Co-exist.

As a non-Fellowship member, *The Ambrose Chronicle* was Ian's only chance to become a reporter. *The Chronicle* served his hometown of Ambrose, Virginia. The next closest city with a newspaper was Lynchburg, a Fellowship town awarded with all kinds of Federal favors.

"Did I tell you?" Seated next to Ian, Montgomery Jones smoothed his compulsory red necktie, one of the latest skinny styles.

Self-conscious, Ian straightened his broader tie, a hand-me-down from his older brother.

"I'm going to the Shaming in Lynchburg tomorrow." Monty laced his fingers together and put his hands behind his head. Ian's best friend, and the second copyboy at *The Chronicle,* Monty aimed to be a star news photographer. He'd never turn down a chance to go on an assignment, not even to a Shaming.

"Yeah, you told me." The tiniest bit of disapproval seeped into Ian's voice. On this one thing, he and Monty disagreed. Strenuously.

The Fellowship meted out Shaming as punishment. Members who "transgressed against the Fellowship and the Prophet" went through the formality of a trial.

Not one of the Shamed Ones received a not guilty verdict. Ever. Chained to the judgment boxes on the courthouse steps, they stood there regardless of the weather. For days. Sometimes weeks.

"I get to bring my camera." Monty's dad had bought him a professional Speed Graphic Press camera. "I might get an uncredited photograph in the spread." Monty's eagerness had to be for the opportunity, not the Shaming. Still, Ian squirmed.

A barbaric practice, the Shamed Ones suffered the jeers and taunts and rotten vegetables flung by *true* Fellowship members. Jaw clenched, Ian managed not to shudder. Taking pictures skated on the thin edge of decency.

One day, as an investigative reporter, Ian would challenge every local, state, and federal law. Nibble at the Fellowship until it disappeared.

"Boy!"

Ian whipped his head around to see who had called.

The Chronicle's feature reporter, Claude Collins, held his arm in the air, summoned him with a snap-of-the-wrist wave.

Flutters stirred in his belly and his mouth went dry. Collins had promised to read an article Ian had written. Ian hurried through the labyrinth of desks.

Crammed into the corner, two filing cabinets, a bookcase, and a typewriter on a roll around stand surrounded Collins. Mountains of old newspapers, a Rolodex, a telephone, and a celluloid Donald Duck nodder crowded his desktop.

The phone rang.

No. Don't take it.

Collins rolled his eyes, took the call.

Of course, he had to take it. Ian stuck his hands behind his back, clamped them together in a sweaty knot. He strained to stand still. Fought the urge to make bug-eyes.

With the receiver captured between the notch of his neck and shoulder, Collins's pencil scratched across a yellow paper pad that wobbled atop a stack of newspapers. "Uh, huh. Yeah. I got that." He stuck the pencil behind his right ear. "I owe you one." He slammed the receiver on its hook and glanced up. "Good, it's you."

"Yes, sir. What can I do for you, sir?"

"First, I told you, don't call me sir." Six-feet tall with perfect posture, thick silvered hair, and impeccable style, Collins made an imposing figure. Though today his tossed aside suit coat, unknotted tie, and newsprint grayed shirt cuffs indicated something had upset him.

"Yes, sir—I mean, Mr. Collins."

"Don't—aw, never mind." At a tap from Collins, the Donald Duck nodder bobbled its head. "Look, kid—Ian, right?"

"Yes, s—Mr. Collins." *Please say you've read my article. Say you liked it. Part of it.*

Collins picked up two typed pages. "This isn't bad—"

Ian sucked in a breath. Hope bubbled up.

"You need to learn to ask more open-ended questions." Collins's eyes locked with his. "Listen more."

All the air inside Ian whooshed out. *He hates it.* "Yes, sir." *He took it to shut me up.*

He handed Ian the pages.

Red ink smothered the page with questions and corrections and comments. A bolt of adrenalin shot through Ian and died in a heated flush at the volume of notes. "Oh—wow—um—" *He spent time on it.* A tingle of hope snuck back in. "Thank you, sir —er—Mr. Collins. I'll rewrite this right away and get it back to you."

"You got potential, but you're green." The pencil came out from behind his ear again, he tapped its eraser on the desktop. "The new journalism school at Lynchburg College is a worthy program. Go to college."

He drew in a quick breath and stared at his shoes. *As if I'd be accepted—or could afford a Fellowship-backed school.* "Someday, sir." *Nothing against Pop but I don't want to be a hardware store clerk. Ever. I'll find a mentor somewhere.*

"You remind me of me as a cub reporter."

Ian gave him a weak smile.

"I'd like to take you on as an intern."

"I understand, sir. I—wait." He could not have heard that right. "You want *me* to be *your* intern?"

Collins laughed. "Yes. I do."

Speechless, he opened and closed his mouth like a beached guppy. Inane words tumbled out of his mouth. "Thank you, sir— Mr. Collins—for the—oh, gosh—I mean—I appreciate the opportunity."

"Intern work is unpaid. You still have to go to school and fulfill your copyboy duties."

"I won't let you down, Mr. Collins."

"Good." He handed him a lumpy five-by-nine manila envelope. "Take this to Leland. Try the dark room." He swiveled to face the typewriter. The shrill ring of his telephone pierced the air. He picked up the phone and raised an eyebrow at Ian. "Well? What are you waiting for?"

Clutching the envelope to his chest, Ian whirled and hurried to the stairs.

Sweet printer's ink permeated the basement. And he breathed it in, reveled in it. *I'm an intern.* His lips curled in an unerasable grin. The raucous clatter and grumble of the press pulsed steadfast and strong. He trotted past a half-dozen storage rooms and supply closets.

Above the darkroom door, a red "Do Not Disturb" light glared. He dropped his package into the wire inbox. The outbox held a flat, nine-by-eleven manila envelope addressed to one of the sports reporters. Copyboys never moved fast enough for Dale. *I'll save myself a lecture. Take that upstairs now.*

A quick about-face slammed him into Collins. Alarm zipped through his veins. "Sorry. I didn't hear you," Ian shouted above the roar and ignored the pang of *something's wrong* in his chest.

Collins quirked his head and gave Ian the kind of look that said *follow me.*

Throat tight, he followed the reporter into a gigantic storage room crammed full of monstrous rolls of newsprint.

When the door closed, the press noises muted to an ominous growl.

Farther back in the room the noise dulled. They wouldn't have to shout.

Collins turned and stepped into Ian's personal space. "That business upstairs? A show for the others."

Hope plunged fast and hard. *I'm not an intern.* He pinched his lips tight.

"I appreciate that you trust me, Ian. But what you're doing isn't safe."

His pulse rocketed and he squeezed Dale's envelope against his chest. *Oh, crap. Did he see me?* "I don't understand."

"Several months ago, I heard rumors. The Fellowship had a secret plan, a program, to crush all resistance. I've seen the signs." After a wary glance around the room, he continued. "They've executed that program."

He's trying to scare me. Keep your body relaxed. Act puzzled. "So?"

"It's no secret that your father caters to non-Fellowship."

Relief took the edge off. *It's Pop's violation of the city ordinance he's worried about.* "Pop always says, 'A person who needs a nail needs a nail. Not a membership card.' Besides, he pays the penalty every year." And the Fellowship turned a blind eye. So did most Fellowship members. The store barely broke even.

"Your family is in danger." His dark, urgent tone made Ian's skin creep.

So I wrote Ditch the Fellowship on the water tower and followed a Fellowship flunkie. That shouldn't-- The man's expression was unreadable but ultra serious. Collins had never ratted out a source for a story. The lump in Ian's throat scratched all the way down. *I'm not a source.*

Collins tugged on his ear lobe. The pencil above his ear bobbed up and down. "I know your father believes the Fellowship is wrong. That its role in government violates the Constitution..."

Don't react.

"Regardless, he's endangered your whole family. Now you— you've written this article. You followed a Fellowship leader?

That's not dangerous. That's an invitation to die. You wrote it for you and your family."

Ian didn't have proof—yet. But too much money ran through Rosehill Dump. He hoped uncovering the truth would tarnish the Fellowship, launch his career, and save his father's hardware store. "The truth shouldn't be dangerous."

"You're right. But it is." He put a hand on Ian's shoulder. "You're too much like me. Young and eager. But you have to be smart. Stop this investigation."

The warmth from Collin's hand spread through Ian and in its wake, searing judgment. *This must be a test.* Ten years ago Collins refused to give up on his story about graft in city hall. Ignored all the threats. And it got reprinted by the *New York Times.*

"You didn't stop." More defiance slipped out than he'd intended.

"Be smarter than me. There are times you have to put on the brakes."

A phony smile on his lips, he recovered the proper tone. "If you say so, sir."

"I'm on your side. But, if you want to be my intern, you *have* to promise me you won't pursue this story."

Ian loosened his arms a bit, hid his right hand under his left elbow and crossed his fingers. "I promise." *I promise, someday I'll expose the Fellowship's corruption.*

That earned him a pat on his shoulder. "Good boy." Collins hooked his thumbs into his gray tweed pants pockets. "I have a Sunday feature planned. First Citizens Bank will celebrate their sixtieth-year next month. How about you come to the interview with me? Tonight at eight o'clock. It's a school night. Do you need to ask your parents' permission?"

Permission. I'm not fired. Wait, I'm not a little kid. I'm eighteen. He inhaled and stopped. Ma would worry and he sure didn't want to get one of those "I'm disappointed in you, son" lectures from Pop. He nodded and tried not to grin.

"No one can know we talked down here. We don't want to risk rousing suspicions."

Uneasiness rippled across Ian's shoulders. He took a couple of steps backward. "I understand." But he didn't. This conversation. The privacy. The implied and overt warnings.

Just before Collins disappeared around a roll of newsprint, he glanced back at Ian. "We'll meet out front at seven-thirty."

"Yes, sir, Mr. Collins."

"Seven-thirty sharp."

Ian strode to the back of the room, past the sentries of towering rolls of newsprint. Whether Collins knew about the water tower or not he'd made his concern about the article clear.

Ian whirled and tromped back. *Have I put everyone in danger?*

Second lap. *I should warn Pop. But there's no place for a private phone call. I could tell the Chief I'm sick and need to go home early but--If I'm sick, I can't work the interview...*

Third lap. *Pop knows. All those hunting and camping trips—Survival lessons.*

Fourth lap. *Collins said rumors. Not fact. Not here. Not now.*

Fifth lap. He blew out a breath. *I'll tell Pop after work—oh, crap—Dale's envelope.*

He raced upstairs and suffered Dale's lazy copyboy tirade.

CHAPTER 2

IAN'S HEART and feet pumped and pumped and pumped. Riding into the wind, his jacket billowed and popped. His fifteen-minute bike ride stretched into an eternity.

He had to make it home while Pop was home for his three o'clock break. A proud-of-you-son smile would be appreciated. But Ian needed him to extend his break. He planned to buy that used, soft-top Porsche in the sales lot. An argument would follow.

A reporter needs a car. When you are a reporter you may get a car. *I'm eighteen.* You live under my roof. *I pay rent. Saved up almost two thousand dollars.* That's your college fund. *If I were 21, a parent signature on the sale wouldn't be required.* Then Pop would say, *wait until you're twenty-one.*

A light touch of his right foot to the asphalt and he slid through the final corner.

Half a block down, Collins dashed from Ian's front porch to his car at the curb. He flashed a weird look back at the house, dove into his old gray Pontiac Super Chief, and roared down the street.

Stunned, Ian skidded to a stop. *What the heck? Why would he...? I'll bet he came to get me for a rush assignment.* His shoulders drooped. *He told them.* He didn't know whether to chase

Collins or run inside and get Ma's permission. Ma won. *She'll know where Collins went.*

He flew down the street and up the drive and leaped off his bike. A practiced flip of his wrists set it against the wall. He glimpsed a sedan shape in the garage. *Pop's still home.*

Balling his ink-stained fingers so they wouldn't touch the white paint, he banged through the back door. "Ma. Pop. I'm home. What did Mr. Collins want?"

They weren't in the kitchen.

The pungent odor of bleach burned his eyes and sinuses. He blinked and grimaced and opened the cookie jar, jammed one in his mouth. Oatmeal-raisin. Crispy edges and soft and gooey on the inside. He palmed two more and turned and froze mid-turn.

A Fellowship tract sat in the middle of their yellow and white melamine table.

Help the Fellowship and your government. Follow the Law. Report transgressions.

Preacher Johnson must've visited again. *He should give up. Ma and Pop will never convert.* Ian wadded up the pamphlet, tossed it in the trash.

"Ma, next time dilute that bleach."

Silence.

Maybe she's next door at the Millers. He'd wait. Mrs. Miller had humiliated him once. She wouldn't get another chance. "Pop?"

In the living room, oily paint fumes killed off the bleach. His gut tightened. *Ma didn't say she planned to repaint today.* Pale yellow walls. Not beige. His heart thudded a bass beat. Their banana green sofa had been moved to the window. New yellow and blue throw pillows sat in the armchairs. A plain brown round coffee table stood in front of the sofa instead of Ma's beloved Art Deco piece.

"Ma?" The word sounded like a sheep's bleat. He held his

breath.

Still no answer.

The bass beat drummed louder. *They're upstairs.* He took the stairs two at a time. Passed his parents' empty room, then back-tracked and gaped at their bed. New blue bedspread and drapes brightened the room. A chill slithered down his spine. No way his frugal, depression-survivor mother spent money on bed cover-ings and curtains when the old ones were serviceable. No way she did all this work in one day. No way these changes meant anything good.

His stomach churned and his palms grew damp. His chest tightened with every step of the short walk down the hall to the bedroom he shared with his older brother. He swallowed hard. He paused at his sixteen-year-old sister's room. Nothing out of place. But Leslie believed everything had a place. Opposite Leslie's room, thirteen year old, Travis and six year old, Kenny shared a room. Impossibly clean, the room held not a single stray toy or game or dirty sock. A catch in Ian's throat made him fight for breath. He reached for the doorknob to his room. Hesitated.

His older brother, Henry Junior, a straight A student, got accepted at Lynchburg College. A freshman, thanks to non-Fellowship tuition he still lived at home. He worked full time at the grocery and could only afford one class a semester. He'd taken today off to cram for a test.

Ian opened the door to their shared bedroom. The hairs on the back of his neck stood.

No Junior.

No stacks of textbooks.

No graphic posters of animal diseases on the wall.

New, colorful patchwork quilts covered their twin beds. Clothes had littered every surface this morning. Not now. Every surface gleamed clean and uncluttered. Junior didn't do that. If it wasn't in a book, Junior didn't notice.

Ian's hands trembled. He reached for the closet doors, folded them open, and gawked at the empty closet. His pulse surged to a tympani drum roll. He gasped for air. *All our clothes—gone.* They said this happened when the Azrael Took someone. *But that's a myth. A boogeyman story.*

He dashed downstairs, seized the knob of the front door, and froze. Didn't know what he'd do if the symbol was there. Still, he had to know. He jerked the door open.

There, burned into the door, dark and deep, a blood-red shield sectioned by a white cross.

His breath caught. *Fellowship believers—Do. Not. Live. Here.*

Hands on his knees, head down, he tried to breathe. Burned wood hit the back of his throat and nose. He retched. Hard and dry.

He straightened and wiped his mouth with the back of his hand. Here, in the door, anyone—everyone—could see him. He slammed the door, whirled, braced his back against it. Sucked air in and out, in and out, in and out. His head spun. *Slower. Need to breathe slower.*

It didn't help.

Ma. Pa. Junior. Taken. It can't be.

Junior's a college kid. He's not a threat. Not to the Fellowship. Not to anyone.

The Second Sphere—didn't bother with the small stuff. The Angel of Death—

He squeezed his eyes shut.

The Angel of Death—Does. Not. *Can not.* Exist.

But the Second Sphere exists.

Collins knew.

Ian fled to the garage and jerked the doors open.

A shiny new 1960 midnight blue four-door Studebaker Champion filled the narrow garage. No pink bike in sight. Ma's bike. She wouldn't bike to the grocery. She'd have Pop drive—

Sharp raw understanding knifed through Ian, ripped his heart open. *Taken. Erased. Dead.* He couldn't breathe, couldn't move, couldn't think. Didn't *want* to think.

The *ooga-ooga* of a bicycle horn wrenched him back to here, now. A young boy in a *Föderation von Deutschland* uniform pedaled past, followed by a half-dozen more young Nazi boys. Ian tensed. Pop hated the steady influx of Nazis tourists after they had won the war. He said, "You scratch a Nazi you'll find the Fellowship up in your business." The same Fellowship that had Taken his parents and Junior.

Taken.

They should have arrested Pop, should have tried him. Ma and Junior had nothing to do with—They didn't do anything wrong.

Someone lied. Someone ratted on the wrong people.

Ian scanned the street, his neighbors' houses. *The Nazi boys? Preacher Johnson? A customer? A neighbor?*

His pulse thrummed like an overstretched guitar string. *Collins said there was a secret plan. A Fellowship program.* They would come for him, too. Not safe. This house—Ambrose—would never again be safe.

He snatched the garage doors shut. *Have to get out of here and hide*—somewhere—the mountains. They hid things for years and years—sometimes forever.

In the dark, he stumbled, then squeezed between the car and the storage shelves. *Please, let my Scouting gear be here.*

It wasn't.

Sunlight filtered by dirty windows and sheer curtains stirred by the breeze cast undulating shadows that crawled across the car and the walls. He didn't dare draw attention, turn on the light. He groped the boxes on the shelves.

On the top shelf, something soft yielded. A rucksack with a sleeping bag inside.

Now for a tarp and some tools...

On the workbench he found a coil of rope, a hatchet, and a hunting knife, but no tarp.

He spun and faced the car. He should steal it. He dashed inside.

On the wall next to the kitchen door hung a wrought iron trivet, not the hooks where his parents hung their car keys. Ian whirled and threw a wild, searching glance around the kitchen.

Creak. The sound came from the front of the house. He tried to tell himself that the wind blew open the door. Wind or not, he didn't wait. He sped back to the garage.

After he stuffed everything into the sleeping bag's rucksack, he swung the strap of the over his shoulder. He pedaled his bike as if he were in a Grand Prix race.

Chaos ruled his thoughts. *It makes no sense. They should have Taken me.* He skidded to a stop. *The newspaper is a public place.*

Ian scanned the park, another public place. The swing sets stood to his right. The ones Kenny played on every day while Leslie made goo-goo eyes at her latest beau.

Leslie's school-work program—she's at the doctor's office—the younger kids at school— Maybe they didn't Take Leslie or Travis or Kenny, either. He glanced at his wristwatch. Leslie would be home soon, then Kenny and Travis would follow. *They don't know.*

The Second Sphere think they can erase the whole Hobart family. He clenched his teeth—hard. *I can't let that happen. I won't let it happen. Ma would never forgive me.* He stashed his gear in a hollow log near the creek, then pumped his legs faster than his heart rate all the way home.

Leslie's sobs pierced him the moment he opened the door. He took the stairs two at a time. "Leslie?"

"Ian?" Her shriek ripped through the air. She flew out of the bathroom and into him. Arms and legs wrapped around him, she buried her face in his shirt.

He held her tight, wanted to punch someone for breaking his little sister's heart.

"The shield..." Her words dissolved into more sobs. Her warm tears wet his shirt.

"Shh. Shh. I know." He fought against the black emptiness inside.

Calmer, she swiped stray brown hairs out of her face. Swollen and bloodshot, her blue eyes searched his. "Ma and Pop?"

He nodded.

She bit her lower lip. "Junior?"

His head dipped and his gaze fell. The spoken words fanned the flames that raced in his veins and something deep inside him hardened.

"What about Ken—" Her lips quivered but no more tears fell.

"Doesn't happen if you're in a public place. Like school."

"Then if Pop's at the store—?"

They raced downstairs to the wall phone in the kitchen. He dialed.

"Logan's Hardware. We got what you need. How may—"

He slammed the receiver into its hook. His lungs heaved air in and out. *Not Hobart's.*

"Maybe you misdialed." Leslie seized the phone.

He slapped the hook down and held it. "I just alerted them that we're here."

Her breath grew ragged. "But if they wanted us, why didn't someone wait at the paper for you and at Doc Bennett's for me?"

"I don't know. Maybe they thought it would be easier here."

She threw a glance toward the front door. "Do you think someone's out there now?"

Of course. But they had to see me leave and come back. They couldn't have but didn't grab me—us— He wobbled, took half step to keep his balance. "They *should* have grabbed us already. Someone made a mistake or—they want us to—I don't know—lead them somewhere." Ian put his cold hand on Leslie's warm shoulder. "Whatever the reason, it gives us a chance. If we're careful."

She sniffled and cleared her throat. "What about Travis and Kenny?"

"If we're still —here—" He licked his lips. "—they are, too. We'll—get them from their schools—Take them with us. Hide."

"Where? They'll search for us everywhere." Leslie's voice shook.

"In the mountains—until we can figure out where to go." *And how I can repay whoever's responsible—* "I've got some gear stashed near the park."

She flung her arms around him again and held him tight. Too tight.

He unpeeled her arms from his neck and led her upstairs. "We'll need blankets."

A frown creased her face the way it did Ma's face when she concentrated. "And food. And coats and a change of clothes..."

"If they left any—Junior's and mine—"

She ran to her bedroom.

"—gone."

Her wail rent the air. She returned to the hallway empty-handed, stared up at him. "What if Mrs. Rules-are-rules won't let us take Travis out of school?"

"We'll call the office. Say Pop's been hurt—" his voice broke.

"We should just tell them the truth."

"We don't dare. Anyone we tell could be the next one Taken."

Her hand flew to her mouth.

"Call the school. Apologize for your sore throat, say you've been crying."

"That part's true." She blew out a breath and squared her shoulders. "Okay."

"Get some blankets, then make the call. I'll find more camping gear. Meet me in the garage." Ian leaped three steps at a time on his way down.

He retrieved the second sleeping bag and did a thorough search. A flashlight, an almost full box of matches, and two canteens went into the second rucksack.

Leslie hurried into the garage. Laden with a couple of colorful patchwork quilts, a thin blanket, and a cloth A&P Grocer's bag full of food, she gaped at the car. "We should take it."

"No keys. Besides," He should have thought of it earlier. "It's a Fellowship car. They recorded make, model, VIN, license —everything."

She bit her lower lip and gave a nod.

"Did you call both schools?"

"I told them you and I would come and pick up Travis, then Kenny." She gave a half-laugh, half-hiccough. "Kenny's school secretary told me to gargle salt water."

"Hurry." Ian helped Leslie roll the quilts into the second sleeping bag. "It's only fifteen minutes until the dismissal bell." They worked together to force the quilt-stuffed sleeping bag back into its rucksack.

The roar of a car engine drew near. Ian exchanged wary glances with Leslie.

He held a finger to his lips, tiptoed to the side door, and opened it a crack. At this angle, he couldn't see the front yard or the street. No ominous stranger in the back yard. No suspicious car in the alley. He waved for Leslie, took her hand, and bolted for the alley.

CHAPTER 3

CAPTAIN JEFFERY WILLIAMS touched the perfect replica of the Sheriff's badge pinned to his suit. He assumed the persona and strode into the building. George Washington Junior High was a maze of painted cement block and uninspired linoleum over concrete. Muted voices hummed behind closed doors. Perfumes, perspiration, and pine floor cleaner filled the air.

A sign labeled office pointed right. The crisp click-clack of his shoes echoed down the hall.

A door banged and a student dashed toward him. Williams halted.

The student waved a hall pass and darted out of sight.

Slow, measured breaths through gritted teeth kept his blood pressure under control.

He flung open the office door. A Captain of the Cleaners division of the Second Sphere shouldn't be reduced to this. He marched to the counter. If he *were* a field agent, he wouldn't work daylight hours, much less walk into a public school.

A woman with a dull brown wad of hair on top of her head beamed a mouthful-of-teeth smile. "Good afternoon. How may I help you?"

"I'm Officer Williams, I need Ian Henry Hobart and his sister, Leslie Annys Hobart, brought here immediately."

"Dismissal is at three o'clock. You can sit over there." She nodded toward three straight-backed wooden chairs set against the wall.

"This can't wait fifteen minutes." Years of practice allowed him to control his tone, conceal his clenched fists.

The woman scratched her head and more hairs escaped her bun. "Where did you say you're from? I don't recognize—"

"I'm from the Chesterfield County Sheriff's Office." An irresistible but grim smile ought to put her at ease. "There's been an accident. Please hurry." The lie rolled off his tongue smooth as glass.

"Oh, my. Was it a bad one?"

"Ma'am, time is of the essence." If she bothered to call for references, she would learn Officer Williams, a trusted civil servant, had served the county for twenty years. He prayed she wouldn't. The delay would complicate the job.

She twisted to face the shelf behind her, dragged out a large black notebook, and dropped it. It thudded onto the counter. "They're good kids. I hope their father is okay. But, you know—"

Find them in the blessed book.

"I don't think either one of them is in class—"

On its own volition, his mouth flew open. He clamped his lips tight against the scream "what?" His stomach bubbled with the suspicion that he'd been given the wrong information—again. Three months ago, his boss had promised to find and punish the man who made the error. This second event meant either Major Banks was maneuvering to get rid of Williams or an office coup was in the works.

The woman leafed through the schedule.

Every page she turned cranked the heat in his stomach closer and closer to a boil.

"Ah, here it is." Her finger tapped a line of tiny type. "They *are* both in the work-experience program."

Alarm stiffened his back. "Out of the school?"

"Of course. He's at the newspaper and she's at Dr. Bennett's. But they should be home any—"

He stormed out of the office and out the front door. *If I'm to survive the office coup, I will have to take the head of the incompetent who did the research.*

The rental, a five-year-old, midnight blue, unmarked Studebaker Hawk waited in the parking lot. *Stupid Second Sphere pencil pusher assumed his shoddy investigation would slide past the lowly Cleaners.*

He slid into the driver's seat, flipped open the map hard enough the paper popped. *The investigator didn't anticipate that I would be on the job.*

Roads crisscrossed the city. The newspaper building and the doctor's office were miles apart. *I'm closer to the paper.* He'd sent Nickerson to the junior high and Adler to the elementary. Yardley was at the house and would have to nab the girl when she got there. A sharp right out of the parking lot and Williams headed downtown. It irked him that not a single Second Sphere cadet was available to replace his aide. Lieutenant Adler always drove. *Instead, I'm driving and he's in the field on a job he hasn't worked for ten years.* Two more pegs in the bad day board.

He snatched the heavy, rectangular two-way radio off the passenger seat then tuned it to the proper channel. The tinny buzz sounded six times. *Answer, Yardley.* Disgusted, Williams tossed the olive drab Handie Talkie. It bounced, then settled on the seat.

He'd demanded his commander request a delay. But the Fellowship Council refused to hold their Purification program until the Cleaners had a larger force.

Not two blocks down the street and he hit a red light.

The Azrael's sole function was to kill the dissidents.

Clean up required more time and, during this Purification, more men than Williams had in the entire division. Stretched to the limit, every member of his department worked assignments. Add to that the inherent risk in removing four children from public schools....

He thumped his fingers on the steering wheel like that would make the stoplight change faster.

Major Banks had every faith the captain would deliver 100% as usual. *Good grief, I'm not a miracle worker.*

Green light.

The car's wheels screeched against the pavement. After an assignment in nearby Wytheville, he and his men had blown into town at 8:30 this morning. *Too many assignments. Too little sleep. Too tired to perform miracles.*

He glared at the stoplight two blocks ahead, willed it to stay green.

Red light.

He slammed on the brakes. *Blasted small town mentality. Stoplights on every blessed corner.*

Cleaners acquired collateral targets, if any, from their beds, *in the dark of the night.* They sedated the unfortunates and then handed them off to the Transport Team. He rubbed his face, loosened his tie.

Green light.

Cleaners never meet the collaterals. On a good day, a snatch and grab of four children in daylight hours without stirring suspicions was darn close to impossible. And the way things were going, this day was anything but good.

The newspaper's receptionist asked him to wait. The Chief was in a meeting. For thirty minutes, Williams endured the stench of ink and being ignored while his blood pressure inched up.

The Editor-in-Chief, a wiry guy with a comb-over, strolled into the lobby.

"I'm Officer Williams." He stood and extended his hand. "I'd like to speak to Ian Hobart."

"The copyboy? I'm afraid he clocked out about an hour ago."

Inside Williams blew a gasket, but outside he continued his stupid sheriff act. "Do you know where he was headed?"

"Home."

"He has a car?"

"A bicycle. But he's been and gone again."

He forced a what-do-you-mean smile despite his sky-high blood pressure. He'd been played. *A deliberate delay.* Another hint that his suspicions were correct. *A snitch warned the Hobart children. And the traitor wants my job—*

"My feature reporter picked Ian up for an interview." He yanked up his sleeve and revealed his watch. "He's with Collins. At the train station—though Mr. Smith's train should have left five minutes ago. Wait a minute—" The Chief tilted his head like he was trying to remember. "Collins would drive him home. He may be there by now."

When the Chief launched into a description of the wealthy investor who had been interviewed, Williams walked out.

He climbed back into the car and headed north. His temples throbbed.

A rust-pocked Chevy truck turned in front of him and forced him to drive slower than the sleepy-small-town speed limit.

A check of his rear view showed that three cars followed him, also stuck behind the gosh-darn pickup. An illegal pass would garner too much attention.

The truck wheezed and chugged and crept down the road.

He ground his teeth. His man watching the house didn't expect one teen, much less two.

He one-handed the Handie Talkie. It buzzed, buzzed, buzzed. He turned it off, tossed it back onto the seat, then pounded the steering wheel. *Yardley, Yardley, Yardley*. If one of the cars behind him honked, he'd blast his horn. But not one horn sounded.

The Chevy turned left a block before Hobart's street.

Two sharp turns later and Williams slewed into the alleyway. He strode through the back door and drew up short.

Cans and boxed cereals littered the kitchen floor. Every cabinet door stood open. Shelves that had held canned goods mere hours ago stood bare. His pulse pummeled his ribs.

"Yardley?"

Silence.

Upstairs, the hall closet door stood open. Linens tumbled to the floor. Bedroom closets and drawers were ajar. "Where are you?"

The boy had been home. He must have recognized the symbol, overpowered Yardley, gathered supplies, then ran—*oh, no. Please, God. Give me a break.*

He raced to the garage and spied the car through the window. He blew out a thank-you prayer.

In three strides he reached the car, snatched up his Handie Talkie and signaled Lieutenant Adler.

The alert buzzed ten times. *This can't be happening.* Adler never ignored a call.

"Hello?" Adler shouted. In the background a siren blared and people were yelling.

"Adler? What's going on?"

"Captain? What did you say? I can't hear—" The alarm in the background stopped "—you. Someone pulled the—"

"Stop shouting, Adler. Tell me you have the child."

"No, sir. That's a negative. The fire alarm went off—I lost them in the crowd."

Williams took two slow, deep breaths to calm himself. "You said them. Who?"

"The oldest, the girl, and my subject."

Blast! If the girl was at the elementary school, where the heck is Yardley? "All hands to the elementary school, now!"

CHAPTER 4

ON THE WAY to the park, Ian's stomach clenched. He scanned the area over and over and over, certain they were being watched. At the park, he made a slow half-turn and scanned again. Three preschoolers shrieked and hooted on the merry-go-round. Engrossed in a conversation, two women perched on a nearby bench. He'd seen them before. Didn't know them.

"Now." He and Leslie darted downhill to the banks of the creek. He crouched, hid behind the embankment. So did she.

His rucksack still lay inside the hollow log. *Thank goodness.* They jammed in the supplies they had brought.

A nearby car's fan belt screeched. A dark Ford sedan inched past the park.

The driver's head did a slow pan of the park. Drifted across Ian. The car lurched. Tires skidded. Ian sucked air, seized Leslie's hand, and ran.

They dashed down allies, cut through yards and flower gardens and green spaces. Behind the baseball field and the tennis courts, they hid behind trees. On the other side of the sports fields stood the two-story brick building labeled George Washington Junior High.

Two-dozen vehicles sat in the parking lot. Ian eyed them. At this distance, the insides of the cars held deep shadows. None of them or all of them could be occupied.

A car door clunked open. A man stood and scanned the street. From his dark glasses and suit, to his bearing, to his quick sure movements, every ounce of him, screamed Second Sphere.

Ian ducked behind a fat tree trunk. "Psst! Hide."

Leslie slipped behind an old oak. "We can't wait," she whispered. "The dismissal bell—"

He held a finger to his lip, held his breath, and peered around the tree.

The man in the suit strode toward the back of the school. His head swiveled back and forth, back and forth. His dark glasses blindly scanned the tennis courts.

Ian jerked his head back. Rough bark scraped across his cheek. He couldn't swallow. He had no spit. Precious seconds ticked past. Ten. Twenty. Thirty.

He couldn't wait any longer. Travis could be snatched any minute. He peered around the trunk. The man in the suit vanished around the far corner of the building. Ian signaled Leslie.

They dashed across the field. Inside, they hurried down a hall that reeked of chalk dust, floor wax, and sweat. The hallway to Travis's room was much longer than Ian remembered.

Leslie gave him a go-ahead nod. He expelled a sharp breath and knocked three times.

Mrs. Remington opened the door a quarter of the way. Her tight bun and prim, navy blue dress, and her ever-present pinched expression unchanged from when she'd been Ian's teacher.

"We're here for Travis," Ian said. "Our father's been injured."

She extended her hand, palm up. "The slip."

"Ma called. They know."

An eyebrow conveyed her disapproval. "You know the rules, Ian Hobart. You *must* have the form from the office."

"Please." He slid his foot over the threshold. "We've got to go to the hospital."

She pruned her lips.

"It's a matter of life and death," Leslie pleaded.

A long-suffering sigh escaped her, and she turned toward the classroom.

Ian pushed the door farther open and searched curious faces. He didn't see his brother.

"Ian?" Travis stood, slung his bright blue book bag over his shoulder, clutched his green jacket in both hands, and sped across the room. "What's wrong?" His gaze darted from Ian to the teacher and back.

Arms crossed, she glared down her nose at Ian. "The office first."

"I'm sorry." Ian reached for Travis.

She stepped between Travis and the door. "There are rules."

"Have you no heart? Our father's hurt. We have to leave. Now!"

"Pop's hurt? Let me out." Travis ducked and wriggled around his teacher and then pushed through the door.

"You'll get a week's suspension for this—or an expulsion."

Ian dragged his brother into a trot. Leslie kept pace.

Behind them, Mrs. Remington fired a command at her students, then stomped down the hall toward the office.

Travis tore free of Ian's hold and ran alongside him. "What happened? How bad is he?" "Will he be all right?"

"Shh," Leslie said. "We'll tell you outside."

"Which hospital?" "Does Ma know?"

Ian didn't answer. The hall telescoped and grew. Sweat beaded on his lip. The skin of his back twitched as if spiders crept down it.

Quick footsteps echoed in the hall behind them. "Hey—you. Stop."

He glanced over his shoulder. Leslie and Travis did, too.

The man in the suit sprinted toward them.

Wide-eyed, Travis didn't need to be told to run faster. "Pop's not hurt, is he?"

Too far from the exit. Need a distraction. His gaze ricocheted around the hall. *There. Hung on the wall.* A red fire alarm.

He snagged Travis by the book bag and Leslie by the hand. Wrenched them to the wall.

"What the heck?" Travis thrashed and flailed. Leslie reached for Travis.

Ian yanked the lever. A shrill alarm whooped.

Classroom doors banged open.

Students filled the hall. Hundreds of shoes and whispers created a dull roar.

Ian tightened his grip on Leslie and Travis and dove into the crowd.

Students and teachers jostled and jolted them. He glanced back. Blocked by dozens of bodies, the man in the suit peered over the students' heads.

Ian plowed forward, fought to stay in the middle of the crowd. They poured through and out the back door. Hurtled around the tennis courts to the grassy baseball diamond.

"Can't stop." Ian dragged them onward, plunged through the outfield, then through the trees and down the next street.

Ahead of him, Travis slowed and peered back at the school. "Where are we going?"

Ian pushed him forward. "Hurry. Kenny needs us."

CHAPTER 5

THEY RAN all ten blocks to the elementary school. Hurried across the exposed playground.

"Don't talk," Ian told Travis between gasps for air. "We'll tell you everything soon."

Travis's glance questioned his sister.

She nodded and ran her fingers across her lips in a close-the-zipper motion.

Travis frowned but kept his mouth shut. They sped into the school and down the hall.

Mrs. Peterson recognized Ian and Leslie. When Ian told her about Pop, she brought Kenny to the door without delay.

Leslie grabbed Kenny by the hand. They hurried four abreast down the hall.

More and more of Ian's muscles tensed. "Faster," he whispered. "Faster."

They rounded one last corner. The glass exit doors stood less than a hundred feet away.

The *tap-tap-tap* of running feet spiked the hairs on the back of his neck. *Need another distraction.* Left—lockers. Right—concrete walls and closed doors. Ahead—on the wall—a fire alarm. *It worked once.*

"Ian Hobart?"

He sprinted forward, scooped Kenny up, and jerked the fire alarm lever.

The alarm shrieked.

Once again, students filled the hallway with a dull roar.

Travis and Leslie banged out the door.

Ian's blood pounded a tempo their feet couldn't match. "Don't stop." "Keep going."

They reached the vacant park. Any minute the schools, recovered from the false alarms, would unleash hundreds of students. Hyperactive, talkative, inquisitive kids would flood the park.

Ian scanned for watchers. None. He herded his siblings down the embankment to the hollow log.

"Why did you say Pop was hurt?" Travis squinted at Ian.

"He's not hurt." A trickle of tears became a cascade down Leslie's cheeks.

Travis gaped at his sister. Suspicion crept over his face and he bounced a black look from Ian to Leslie and back. "I'm not taking another step until you tell me what's going on." He stood in an angry Mighty Mouse pose, arms crossed over his chest.

The confusion on Kenny's face lightened. He pushed his lower lip out and took a mini-Mighty Mouse stance. "Me too."

"We don't have time." Ian dragged bags out of the log.

"They don't understand," Leslie reminded him.

He scowled at his brothers. They scowled back. Sigh. "Get down. I'll tell you." He knelt on one knee.

The boys each took a knee. Leslie knelt close to Kenny. They formed a semi-circle around him. All three looked up at him. For answers. His chest hollowed out and his throat tightened. He pushed his rattled emotions into a mental closet and locked the door.

Quickly and quietly, he told them about the changed house and the symbol.

"They're dead?" Travis's voice cracked, ended an octave higher.

Ian peered over the embankment. A whimper drew his attention back to his youngest brother.

Kenny's chin quivered. "No—" He took a shaky breath. "Pop's—at the—store." His shoulders bobbed up and down, up and down. "Ma, too. Right?" Clouded, his eyes sought Leslie's.

She rubbed Kenny's back. "I saw the symbol, too. And—we called the store—they're gone. Ma, Pop, Junior—were Taken." He buried his face in her shoulder.

Ian glanced away. Focused on the empty swings.

"Are we—" Travis glanced right then left.

"Yeah. We have to get out of here." Ian forced himself to keep his voice down. "The Fellowship won't want us around, reminding everyone."

"Why? They didn't do anything—" Travis's expression twisted Ian's gut.

He glared at the street.

Travis clenched his fists and shook his head back and forth. "We can't let them get away with—"

"I know." Ian made his voice flat and hard. "But those men at the school? Both schools? They want to catch us. We can't let that happen." He grabbed the fattest rucksack and thrust it at Travis. "Ma would want us to survive." Held it mid-air. "All of us." Searched the park again.

Leslie wiped Kenny's tears with her fingers, then stood. She lifted the A&P bag and offered Kenny a sad smile and her hand. He took it. They started toward the mountains.

After several deep breaths, Travis shed his bright blue school bag, kicked it toward the hollow log, and then shrugged the rucksack on.

Ian caught the school bag and rifled through the books, note-books, pens, pencils, comb. *Nothing we can use.* A hand reached around him, grabbed the comb.

Travis shoved the comb in his back pocket, turned, and followed Leslie.

Ian scooped up the second rucksack and scanned the park one last time.

He trotted to catch up with his siblings.

———

Hunched between tall mountain laurel hedges and the side of a sprawling Victorian-style house, Ian watched a midnight blue Studebaker crawl toward them—again. The driver peered out, searched the houses.

He glanced over his shoulder through withered brown leaves. The others had hidden well. Hot and tired and terrified, their eyes fixed on him. They counted on him, the oldest, to keep them safe. His stomach twisted. *The oldest—now.* His mind skittered away from that.

Must stay in control. Control means survival.

Stalked by the Studebaker and the gray Ford from the park, they'd spent more time in bushes and ditches than walking. In two and a half hours they had crossed maybe three miles.

The Studebaker drove out of sight. Ian wriggled out from the bush, signaled the others.

They walked westward.

"We can't go to the hunting cabin, can we?" Leslie's hoarse voice belonged to a stranger.

No. Too dangerous. Everyplace is dangerous. Except—the cave...

"Why not?" Travis asked.

"Too many people know about it." No one else had ever found the cave.

"Our friends wouldn't—"

He shot Travis an are-you-serious glower.

"Then where are we going?" Travis's tremulous tone betrayed his sullen expression.

"We could go to that abandoned house in the field of wild-flowers," Leslie suggested.

"Too close to the cabin." He'd never told anyone about the cave he found during a hunting trip.

The familiar squeal of a fan belt boosted Ian's pulse. "Hide."

He pointed. His siblings dove through a hedge that edged a yard. He followed and lay flat on his belly like his siblings.

The squeal inched closer and closer. Through the tangle of stems, the lower third of the dark gray Ford pulled up even with his position and stopped.

The Ford from the park. Ian held his breath and tried to sink lower into the dirt. He sent desperate mental messages to his siblings. *Be invisible. Don't move. Don't breathe.*

The squeal climbed the scale to ear piercing and moved on.

Ian blew out a deep breath, cleared his head.

At least two cars of agents searched for them, maybe more. Gotta move faster. Gotta to get to the mountains. To the cave.

He peered over the bushes. No sign the cars he knew searched for them. Several other cars sped past. Startled, he glanced at his watch. *Oh, no.* Rush hour—when any car could be the one that spotted them. He herded his siblings away from the main road and sidewalks.

Swivel, scan, walk. He led the way. The others fell into line, Leslie, followed by Travis then Kenny. No matter how he urged them, they progressed no faster than an inchworm.

He had to get them to the mountains. But there were miles of road to walk and dozens of nosy people to pass before they could get there.

"How much further?" Travis asked, surly and snappish.

More than exhausted, Ian grumbled, "A long way." *At least nine more miles.*

"A long way?" Leslie mocked his tone. "You don't know where we're going, do you?"

"We're going to the mountains."

"All of them? Or one in particular?" Her sarcasm dripped with false sweetness.

The urge to smack her balled his hands. She deserved a smack to the back of her head. "I found a cave a while back. It's deep enough in the forest, no one will find us."

"Deep like the ocean?"

He gritted his teeth. *Gotta survive.* He ratcheted down his irritation. "Quit bellyaching. We haven't even gotten to—" *Holy mackerel. Monty.* "—the city limits."

A testy silence followed.

I should have thought of Monty before. Best friends since kindergarten, they had gotten one another out of scrapes plenty of times. *No, I can't—his life—his family would be at risk. Better for all of us if we keep walking.*

The sun dropped behind the mountains and house lights and streetlights blinked on.

Kenny trailed so far behind that Leslie fell back and took his hand again.

A block before Monty's street, Leslie whispered, "Hide."

They dashed for the foundation planting of waist-high evergreens, took cover in a piney scent and sticky needles.

The Studebaker stole toward them like a Saturday night crawl down Main Street. Passed them so slowly Ian's heart faltered. Finally, it entered the intersection and turned.

The car vanished and Ian counted to sixty before he stood.

The others followed him out of the bushes. He brushed at the hundreds of dead pine needles stuck in his clothes.

"You guys are walking bushes—" Kenny giggled. "Me, too. Ow. It scratches."

Leslie stopped and pulled pine needles out of Kenny's shirt.

"We can't stop," Ian said.

She quirked her mouth and side-glanced at Kenny who held his shirt out. "Ow-ow-ow."

At this rate, they wouldn't arrive at the path to the cave for at least another six hours.

Ian and Leslie plucked dead pine needles out of Kenny's shirt in quick jerky movements. Finally, they resumed their trek. No one spoke. Too lost. Too tired. Too frayed.

Ian's burning feet grew heavy and the rucksack gouged his shoulders. His pace slowed. *Can't stop.* Every minute in town meant a chance they couldn't hide well enough, a chance they couldn't run fast enough, a chance they couldn't evade the Fellowship member who'd report them. *Heck. Ma would stop a bunch of kids walking alone at night.*

"We should have hot-wired the car in the garage." Leslie's morose statement startled him.

"Scouts didn't teach me auto theft. Did you learn it?"

"No." The quiver in her voice doubled the weight of the rucksack he carried.

She's right. We're too slow. The Second Sphere will catch us. For a split second, he considered striking out on his own.

Selfish. A heavy sigh escaped him. His selfishness had gotten them into this mess. *The stupid water tower. My article... Collins* — His shoulders twitched. He should have called Pop. It might have saved them. But the interview had been more important. Inside him, a yawning hole split open.

"I'm starved. Do we have anything to eat?"

Only Travis would think of food right now. "We can't stop."

Leslie blew out a huffy breath. She kept pace and fished two hotdogs out of the A&P sack. Handed one to Travis, the other to Kenny.

Their pace slowed to a plod. Ian's nerves twitched with must-go-faster urgency. A mile inside the forest, they'd be harder to find. There they could walk at Kenny's speed.

They needed a lift.

Can't call a taxi. Can't knock on a random door. Can't call a friend—

No. He *could* call Monty. Monty would do it—regardless of his own risk and he'd never give up their secret.

If I ask him this, I'll never ask anything else. I'll never put him at risk again.

He passed Monty's street. At the next corner, he turned and led his brothers and sister to the south side of a worn garage beside an old farmhouse, the one behind Monty's home. "You guys wait here. I'm gonna see if Monty can give us a ride a ways up the mountain."

"We can't wait here." Bug-eyed, Travis jutted his chin toward the house. "Somebody lives there. They'll see us."

"Listen," Ian said.

Above the crickets chirping came the muffled CBS Nightly News theme song.

"Monty mows the old lady's yard. He says she can't hear unless she turns the sound all the way up. And she does. Every night. She's well nigh blind, too. She'll never know you're here." He took a step toward her back yard.

"Monty and his folks know us. Let us go with you." Leslie scanned his face then the shadows around them.

"We can't put more people in danger."

She shot him a pained expression, wrenched her gaze away, then scrutinized the shadows.

"I'll be back in three, four minutes, tops."

When she and Kenny and Travis had settled on the ground beside the garage, he crept into the shadows.

Monty lived in an old, two-story Georgia Colonial brick house with a widow's walk on the roof. His parents never locked the front door. But he and Ian never used it. Their secret, after-dark adventures always started with a climb out of Monty's second-floor bedroom window.

Ian plucked three pebbles out of the flowerbed next to Monty's back door, then hurried back to the old oak.

The tree sheltered the yard with thick outstretched branches that brushed the sides and roof of the house. An overhead light shone in Monty's window and cast a Monty shaped shadow. He sat at his desk, head down, reading or writing.

A lump in Ian's throat threatened to choke him. He bit his lip, hard. *This will be the last time I ever do this.*

He tossed the pebbles, one at a time, against the window.

Shadow Monty straightened up at the first ping of a pebble on the glass. After the third ping, he opened the window and leaned out.

Ian waved.

Monty climbed out of his window—stretched and reached and pulled himself up and over the balustrade. He hurried to the huge tree branch that reached over the roof. Moments later he stood in front of Ian. "What's up?"

"Ma—Pop—Junior—the symbol..." Ian pressed his fists against his forehead and gulped air until the pain released his throat. He dropped his fist and the words spilled out. "They're dead. We gotta hide."

Monty's eyes widened, his jaw dropped. "I—I don't know what to say—"

"Don't say anything." One sappy or kind word would shatter his control. "You gotta help. Take us up to Quarry View Road."

"You're gonna hide at the Quarry?" Monty gave him an are-you-for-real squint.

"Take us to the *road*. Stop. We get out. And you get to come back home." Crisp and cold and achingly resentful.

"But—"

"No. No questions." Forceful, final. "The less you know the better."

"Where are your supplies and food and—and—shelter?"

I don't know. Too many I don't knows. "We'll make do."

"I can bring you what you need. Information, too."

Ian's chest tightened at his friend's generosity, but he shook his head. "It's too risky. You risk—everything—talking to me. I wouldn't ask but I'm desperate."

Monty's face furrowed in a thoughtful frown. "Mom and Dad will want to know why I want to borrow the car at this hour."

The wind sailed out of Ian like he'd been punched. His knees threatened to buckle. *We're on our own. Truly alone.* Inside, the darkness, the void grew. "That's okay, Monty. I'll figure this out —" He turned to leave.

"Wait." Monty grabbed his arm.

The warmth of the hand on his arm penetrated the sleeve of Ian's windbreaker. Surprised, Ian gawked at Monty's hand. He hadn't realized he was cold.

Monty released him, fingers splayed. His hand hovered over Ian's arm a moment before Monty stuck it in his pocket. "I didn't say I couldn't do it. I'll tell them—I left my history book at the newspaper."

"Did you?"

Monty rolled his eyes. "Nah. But it'll give me twenty minutes to get you guys up the road." He glanced behind Ian. "Where is Kenny and—"

Tempted to look toward the old lady's house, Ian focused on

Monty's house. In the stiff breeze, the old oak's shadow waved skeletal limbs in a macabre dance across Monty's window. "We'll meet you in front of Old Lady Scott's house in five minutes."

"Five minutes."

After Monty had climbed back into his window and the bedroom light went out, Ian watched the tree limbs whipped by the cold wind. Colder than he'd realized, the wind filled his unzipped jacket. *Not good. Not paying enough attention. That'll get me, us, killed.* He zipped his jacket and hustled back to where he'd left Leslie and the others.

He found them each chewing on another cold hot dog.

Leslie offered him one.

"Not now. Pack up," Ian said. "We have a ride."

A two-tone green 1960 Rambler with Monty at the wheel, pulled up in front of the old lady's house.

Ian hustled everyone into the back seat. "Stay low. Heads below the windows all the time. No one can see us."

A Motorola Handie Talkie and Monty's history book lay on the front seat. He picked them up, climbed into the seat, and slid down until his head was below the window.

Monty shifted into first gear and pulled out. "You want me to drive to the Quarry?"

"Don't talk," Ian said. "If anyone sees you, they'll be suspicious. Stop at the intersection. Don't turn. We'll get out. Then leave."

"I've been thinking about this—" Eyes on the road, Monty spoke through his teeth. "Take the Handie Talkie. You can call me any time. Use our old call signs."

Ian hefted the two-way radio. "It's too big and heavy. Besides I can't put you in—"

"Call me—anytime. I'll meet you at the GTH."

They were ten when they'd built the Green Tree House.

Built it out of scrap lumber and painted it with found green paint., it was their secret place.

"You don't have to use it if you don't want. Carry it. Then all you have to do is—"

"If it'll shut you up, I'll take it." Ian clipped the Handie Talkie to his belt, slid it to a more comfortable position at his side. "No more talking."

Hooking his thumbs under the steering wheel, Monty wiggled his fingers in surrender. The car whined against an uphill grade.

Blinded to traffic and to their pursuers, Ian tried to ignore his helplessness. Thirty minutes of bracing for bumps and dips and turns wrung him out.

Monty pulled over to the side of the road.

The four of them piled out.

Ian leaned in the open window. "I owe you, man. Thanks." He tapped on the roof. "Go."

Monty shot him a concerned look, then set the car in motion. The Rambler and the whine of its engine faded away.

Ian helped Leslie with Kenny who'd fallen asleep. Travis shrugged on the fattest rucksack. Ian slung the other one over one shoulder and grabbed the A&P sack. Then he led them into the cold, dark forest.

CHAPTER 6

WILLIAMS CLIMBED INTO THE STUDEBAKER, folded his arms over the top of the steering wheel, and glared out the windshield. He was hot and tired and flummoxed.

A mix of tall pines and leafless trees blanketed the mountains and dotted the haze-filled valleys that surrounded him. He tried to divine their secrets. But they concealed minutes-old trails as well as they kept hundred-year-old secrets.

His six-year-old would have pitched a fit before walking this far. But his gut told him that the Hobarts would come to the mountain to disappear. It's what he would have done.

If his targets had entered this immense blue-green maze of craggy rocks, creeks, and trails—he was in trouble.

A click then static filled the air. A voice broke through, "Banks Zero Niner calling. Come in."

He raised the handset to his ear and held down the PTT button. "Williams. Go ahead."

"Captain, did I miss your report?" The deep rumble of Major Banks's voice was unmistakable despite the "in-a-tunnel" sound of the Handie Talkie.

"Sir." Williams squared his shoulders. "I haven't had the—opportunity to send it."

"Tell me what I don't know, Captain." His dry tone held the hint of a threat.

Tension crept up his spine. He rolled his neck to relax his throat and vocal cords. "The shipment to Redemption has been delayed."

"Delayed, not canceled?"

"Not canceled."

"This is unlike you, Captain. Has there been a catastrophe I don't know about?"

"The packages were not where they were supposed to be."

"Where they were doesn't matter. Where are they now?"

His grip on the sun-warmed handset tightened. "Twenty-two hours ago, an observer spotted them headed in a northwest direction. They carried camping gear. We patrolled neighborhoods up to the edge of the forest all night. This morning we advanced to the mountain roads. There has been no further sign of them."

The wind-in-a-tunnel sound meant silence on the other end of the line. A sound more ominous than the worst chewing out the Major ever gave a recruit. Sweat beaded on Williams' upper lip.

"Those packages must be found and delivered with no blowback. None. Do you copy?"

"To accomplish that I need a battalion of agents trained in pursuit."

"Are you saying that the packages have more resources than your team? Perhaps you think the packages, despite their tender ages, are smarter?"

"The territory is 800 square miles of forested mountains. Impossible for four men to cover alone."

"Then your men will have to do the impossible, won't they?"

The abrupt silence of the wind-in-the-tunnel signaled that Banks had disconnected. Williams stared through the Handie Talkie. His hollowed-out gut sank to his toes. *You are setting me up, Major. If the rumors are true, one failed assignment equals a visit from Azrael.*

He took a long breath in then out. He had no choice. Time to make the impossible possible. He tuned the radio. "Calling Adler Seven Seven Two One."

"Go ahead."

"I need a complete dossier on the Hobarts and set a meeting with the high school principal—"

"You have an appointment with him in an hour."

"My cover?"

"You're a recruiter for The College of William and Mary in Williamsburg. An alumnus told you about Hobart. One of our sleepers, the alumnus will vouch for you."

Williams rubbed the sandpaper-stubble on his jaw. "I'll need to freshen up."

"I've set up temporary quarters in an abandoned church. You'll find all that you need there, sir."

Williams got directions. Thirty minutes later, he turned off highway 610 onto an unmarked gravel road. Overgrown trees and shrubs hid him from the street long before he reached a battered marquee that read, Sout_ Ridg_w_y Bapt___ Ch_r_h.

The church's white steeple had faded to a gray ghost of itself. The brick walls had wounds of red dust and debris littered the grounds.

Inside the foyer, his aide, Lieutenant Adler, snapped to attention and saluted.

He returned the salute. "At ease."

The intact roof and freshly swept floor made the foyer tolerable. Uneven light glowed from a kerosene lamp placed on a small table with a wooden pew behind it. The table sat next to the sanctuary's double doors.

"We've no power, but there is running water."

He pointed his chin. "My desk?"

Adler's eyes flicked that direction and back. "Mine, sir. Yours is in there."

"The sanctuary," he said dryly. "Why not one of these offices?"

"They are less than habitable."

He opened the nearest door. The stench of mold hit him like a brick. Broken furniture, moldy books, and the tattered remains of choir robes littered the room. He pulled the door closed. "Very well."

"You wanted to clean up." Adler led him down the hall and gestured at his other clean suit that hung on the door to a lavatory.

He strode into the tiny washroom and turned on the faucet. Water brown with rust ran into the sink. He let it run.

Adler stood outside the doorway, shouted over the water. "I have Hobart's school records."

"Go ahead."

"A solid B student, near-perfect attendance record, an Eagle Scout, four years on the yearbook, and two years at the Ambrose Chronicle."

The water cleared. Williams stripped off his sweat and mud infused clothes. "Set an appointment with—"

"You'll see the Scout Master at five, after the principal. And the manager of the paper at eight."

"So late?" He found the soap and washcloth and scrubbed his face and neck and arms. Bathed the lower half, too. The cold water invigorated him.

"He wouldn't see you before he 'put the paper to bed.' His words, sir. I didn't insist—"

"Yes, yes. You did the right thing. The, um, manager isn't also the Editor-in-Chief, is he?" Perhaps he'd have Adler—

"No, sir." Adler cleared his throat. "Sir, may I ask an impertinent question?"

"Cut to the chase, Lieutenant."

"Shouldn't we reach out to the sleepers here in Ambrose?"

One arm in the clean shirt, an internal shudder rippled through him. He took a long, measured breath. The devil would hold an ice cream social in hell before he'd invite the deceit of a sleeper like his uncle into an investigation. *His* investigation.

He released his breath over a longer measure, adjusted his shoulders, and slipped the shirt on. Fortunately, Adler hadn't noticed his pause.

No one could know how that word affected him. Sleepers. Bile bubbled and twisted in his gut.

Suit coat on, he adjusted his tie and buried his contempt. "Is it worth the risk to jeopardize our sleepers' covers over four *children*? Do you doubt we will apprehend them?"

Adler straightened, more at attention than at ease. "No, sir. You're right, of course."

Williams checked his image in the splotchy mirror. Calm. Capable. Controlled. He glanced at his watch and raised an eyebrow.

"I'll get the car, sir."

CHAPTER 7

HIDDEN IN A PINE GROVE, Ian kept watch over his sleeping siblings. He couldn't sleep, couldn't close his eyes. If he did, he'd fall into the bottomless gorge that had settled inside him. A gorge with sheer rock walls so deep and so wide he couldn't see the other side.

Ma—Pop—Junior—Taken. Gone. Departed. Passed-on. The gorge echoed over and over and over again. He'd said it once, to Monty. Yet, now—

If you didn't say the word you could pretend they were—not here—but somewhere.

But *somewhere* was a lie. Pop once told him that not one person who had been Taken had reappeared—anywhere—ever.

The truth shouldn't hurt so much. They're... Pain corkscrewed deeper.

Ma, Pop, and Junior—are dead.

Final and heavy, the word dead promised him peace if he'd allow it to pull him down into the gorge where he never had to move again. It tempted him, but his promise came first. When the others were safe....

Dawn's weak sunlight didn't warm him or chase away the

hollowness inside. Bone tired, he woke the others. They broke camp and ate PB&J sandwiches on the trail.

They trudged single file up narrow animal trails that wound around rocks and bushes and trees. No one spoke a word and that suited Ian.

They entered a meadow and Leslie drew even with him. "Where are we going?"

Travis joined them. "I still think we should go to Pop's cabin."

"We're going to the cave I found."

"But—"

"We can't—endanger—anyone else." *Or let them endanger us.*

They walked in silence again. A cool breeze swirled dry leaves in eddies that rustled and whispered.

The spiders that had taken permanent residence on his back stirred again. He swiveled and scanned. "Where's Kenny?"

"Here." Kenny lagged about twenty feet behind. On his hands and knees with his nose close to the ground, he studied an anthill.

Ian trotted back to Kenny and took his hand. "You gotta keep up."

"I am." But he walked faster.

Leslie rubbed the back of her neck and raised her face to the sky. "Those are rain clouds. How far to the cave?"

Black clouds scudded under larger, dark gray clouds over-head and the air had that just-before-rain smell. *Crap.* "Rain won't cause any of us to melt."

She huffed. "Of course not. You know that's not what I meant. We need shelter. We don't have dry clothes to change into."

He kicked a loose rock. *What does she want me to say?* "We don't have a lot of things."

"So, what's your plan? We get to the cave, then what?"

"How should I know? I'm winging it here."

"We aren't going to stay in a cave all winter, are we?"

"I don't know." The cave would keep them dry and safe for a while. But food and warmth —at the beginning of November— would be difficult. Nighttime temps already fell close to freezing. There hadn't been a freeze in Ambrose, yet. The weather would turn soon. And winter in the mountains could be deadly.

"We'll have to buy food and clothes," Leslie said. "Not in Ambrose, of course. Big Island maybe? Do you have any money?"

Travis pulled his comb and lint out of his pockets.

A tube of lip balm came out of one of Leslie's pockets and a folded paycheck out of the other.

"You can't cash that. The issuing bank will be notified." Ian reached for his wallet. Patted his empty pockets in disbelief. He had no idea where or when he'd taken his wallet out. He clenched his fists. They literally had nothing but what they carried. Some rescuer he'd turned out to be.

Leslie's damp and over bright eyes and Travis's jerky movements broadcast their belief, we won't survive.

"Don't worry," Travis said. "Pop taught us to hunt. And Ian and I are Scouts—we'll have rabbit stew and fur coats."

Ian side-eyed Travis. *When did he become Mr. Positive?*

"How long will they search for us?" Leslie used her practical voice.

The gorge that hollowed Ian out, widened. "I don't know." Forever. If they had any hope of escape, they needed new identities. For that, they needed money and a forger to make fake IDs. Ian chewed his lower lip. He had no idea where— *The rebels have to know how to do that stuff.* But he didn't know how to find them, either.

"We'll have to find jobs. I can work in a doctor's office and you can work in a newspaper. Far away from Ambrose. Farther away than Big Island..."

"I'm sure they know about the jobs we had, Leslie. We'll have to find new ones." Another reason he had to find the rebels.

"Right." She tugged her skirt free from a thorny bush.

"We could hide in the George Washington National Forest." Travis's voice cracked.

"That's sixty miles away."

"Buena Vista is too far too, isn't it?" Leslie voiced his idea of their best destination.

"It's forty miles by car. But we won't be going by car."

"How long to walk?"

"Cross country it'll be at least six days hard walking." And they'd have to carry or hope they found—food, water, and shelter.

Morose silence followed.

The silence hurt Ian worse than the hollowness inside. He couldn't let Ma and Pop down. He wouldn't let his siblings down. Putting on a cheerful smile and an enthusiastic voice, he said, "Don't worry, guys. Travis is right—between what Pop taught us and Scouts we'll find everything we need." He walked backward and gave them a double thumbs-up gesture. "We can do this. We're Hobarts."

"It'll be an adventure." She didn't sound any more genuine than he did.

He concentrated on finding a safe path up the mountain.

The clouds overhead thickened and darkened the sky.

In the dim light, it grew harder and harder to find the trails. Rocks covered with a thin layer of dry brown leaves threatened to twist an ankle. Branches poked and snagged their clothing.

A breeze brought a damp chill full of the promise of rain. He pushed them faster and faster. Make it to the cave became his silent mantra.

"My feet hurt. I don't wanna go campin' anymore." Kenny's voice scraped across his nerves like fingernails on a chalkboard.

Ian ground his teeth. Focused on the next step, the next path. *Gotta make it to the cave.*

Two minutes later. "Let's go home. I'm tired. And hungry. I want some bacon and eggs, and biscuits, and milk."

"You're six, not two." Travis's peevishness proved him younger than his years, too.

"I wanna go home."

Travis whirled on Kenny. "We can't go home—never ever!"

Kenny's lower lip trembled. "But I'm hungry and tired and cold." Tears flowed down his cheeks.

"We'll warm up in the cave." Leslie took his hand.

A flash of lightning backlit the clouds. *Great. No umbrellas. Can't wait to hear the complaints about getting wet.* He doubled their pace. The sooner they got to the cave, the better.

Travis attacked every branch that dared to get in his way.

The occasional sob disguised as a cough belonged to Leslie.

And Kenny sniffled and sighed and scuffed through the dirt and leaves.

Ian ignored all that and told them to walk faster. They had to make it to the cave.

The rain started, not with drops, but a deluge that soaked their clothes and chilled their skin. Drips from drenched trees made a counterpoint to the pitter-patter of steady rain. They slogged through wet undergrowth and mud. Ian made them walk and eat. Lukewarm cheese and soggy crackers didn't fill anyone's stomach.

A couple of hours later, the rain stopped. They walked on in miserable silence.

He-haw.

Ian froze for a half-second, then herded everyone into the bushes. They crouched and waited.

A second *he-haw* sounded closer. His mouth went cracker dry and lemon sour. *We can't outrun mules. Heck, they walk faster, too. If Second Sphere agents are on mules, how do I protect the others?*

The mule snorted.

His pulse battered his ribs. *It's close. Too close.* He tapped Leslie's shoulder and mouthed, "stay."

He crept toward the approaching mule. He would draw the agents far from his sister and brothers. There—a path, wide enough for a mule to pass. He hunched behind a bush, ready to sprint.

A raspy woman's voice rose above the snort and wheeze of the mule. "Dang it, Frank. Ye know where we be goin'. We been a goin' there near fifty year. Giddyap."

A black mule with one white foot plodded into view. Astride the mule sat an old woman with dove gray braids. She wore an orange plaid shirt and bright green slacks and had a fireman's ax in a holster on her hip. *A hill woman...Alone.*

Not Fellowship. Not Second Sphere. Tension melted from Ian's muscles. His legs shook. *I should ask her for help.* But isolationists to the core and super suspicious, hill people rarely talked to strangers. *And she carries a big ax.*

He slipped back, away from the trail.

The mule slowed near where he had hidden.

"Git on, Frank. Git." The mule snorted and walked forward at a faster clip.

Ian waited until the mule and its rider were out of earshot then returned to Leslie and his brothers. "A mountain woman. She didn't see us. We can go now."

Travis shrugged on his rucksack and Leslie picked up the A&P bag.

"Do we half-ta walk more?" Kenny's shoulders drooped.

He had such a long face Ian relented. "If Les will carry this —" He slipped off the rucksack and handed it to Leslie. "I'll give you a piggyback ride for a while."

It didn't take long before he wished he were the six-year-old carried piggyback. Miserable, chilled through and through, his feet sunk deeper into the mud, made each foot heavier and heavier. His legs ached and his feet burned, but the prickles that ran up and down his back warned of something-bad-coming. He couldn't stop—wouldn't stop—wouldn't let any of them stop.

A cold drop of rain hit his forehead, dripped down his face. *Not again. We deserve at least one break.* Soon random drops grew to a constant light rain.

After a while, the sprinkle became a foggy drizzle. They plodded on cloaked in misery.

The faint light that penetrated the clouds winked out. The dark chilled and disoriented Ian. Without moon or stars or map they could become lost. Deadly lost. A tingle of numbness spread from his teeth to his toes. "Time to walk, Kenny." Ian helped his youngest brother down off his shoulders. "Everyone hold hands." He switched on the flashlight and led the way.

Dark in the woods was a different kind of dark—darker, scarier, lonelier—than when you went hunting with your Pop. He shivered in the falling temperatures and stopped long enough to have the others wrap up in a quilt or sleeping bag. He used the thin, ragged blanket.

A creek gurgled nearby, sent a shot of energy through him. He followed it. The flashlight's bright beam faded at the edges of its cone and cast eerie shadows. In those shadows, the once-familiar bend in the creek became a strange and creepy land. He hoped this was the place. He prayed this was the place. This had to be the place.

He played the flashlight over the trees. West of the creek a rocky bluff rose up into the darkness. He dragged his siblings toward the bluff. The darkness around the flashlight, around them, deepened.

"Leslie, take this." He shoved the flashlight at her. "Point here." He clapped the rock to indicate where. The light didn't help. Both his hands swept over the rock, this way then that. Finally, his fingers found the crack between the rocks. Ian shrugged the rucksack off and took the flashlight back.

"You're going to leave us alone in the dark?" Kenny's voice trembled.

Ian sighed. "I have to. Just for a minute or two."

"Hold my hand," Leslie said. "We'll be okay."

Ian squirmed through the four-foot-long fissure.

The tunnel opened to a rough rectangle, five-by-six feet. He stood. The flashlight pierced the lightless space a beam at a time. The cool dry air couldn't be much above fifty, but that was warmer than outside. He swept his light back and forth across the floor. His shoe prints from more than a year ago pocked the sandy soil. No other footsteps or paw prints disturbed the floor. It would make a safe place to camp—for now.

He left the cave and urged the others to get inside.

They dragged the rucksacks and grocery bag behind them.

They were cold and hungry and grumpy, but they were out of the wet.

Their damp quilts and sleeping bags provided little warmth. They took comfort consuming the last of the peanut butter. It quieted their grumbling stomachs.

Travis laid down at the farthest edge of the light, away from everyone else.

Leslie and Kenny huddled in the middle under a damp quilt. Their teeth chattered and chills shook them.

Ian dropped wearily near the cave entrance. No one, not even Kenny, complained or cried when he turned off the light.

He crossed his legs, propped his elbows on his knees, his chin on his fists. Someone had to watch for the dangerous two-legged predators.

One-by-one the others fell asleep. The chorus of their soft

snores lulled him. His heavy eyelids drifted closed for a second, then two, then exhaustion overtook him. In his dreams, he ran, searched for help, but his friends morphed into Second Sphere agents who captured him. They forced him to watch helplessly while Leslie and Travis and Kenny were Taken by faceless dark angels.

CHAPTER 8

THE SUN'S cold rays chased away the disquiet of Ian's nightmares. Yesterday he believed that if they got to the cave, they'd be safe. He stared at the bubbling creek in front of him and knew they weren't safe. Would never be safe again. Because of him. The hole in Ian's chest grew.

Caught in the turbulent creek, a curled brown leaf bashed against the rocks then hurtled downstream.

"I know Scouts taught you a lot, but we're just kids, Ian."

Startled, he swallowed the shout that tried to escape and tried to still his fright-sped heart. Her stealth approach shook him. He had to be more aware. If she had been Second Sphere...

Leslie stopped at the water's edge wrapped her arms around herself as if to keep from falling apart and stared across the creek.

His chin dipped to his chest. He should have listened to Collins. He should have called Pop right away. If she knew, she would never forgive him.

"We shouldn't have to be out here—hiding." She searched the opposite shore, glanced right then left. "Did you get up early to set some traps this morning?"

He blinked at her. "No."

"I'll help you."

"No time. We'll ration our food."

"But we can't ration food we don't have."

"Won't do us any good to trap food if we're caught."

She put her hands on her hips. "Won't do any good to escape if we starve to death."

"We don't have enough time or the right bait to trap now. When we set up a permanent camp, we will set traps."

"*When* we set up a permanent camp? We aren't staying *here* for a while?"

"We talked about this yesterday. We're going to Buena Vista."

"You expect us to walk again today? All day?"

He gaped at her. "You expected not to?

She propped her fists on her hips and glared. "We need at least a couple of days to rest and recover."

"We're too close to Ambrose. Every day we stay increases our chances of being caught."

"We need dry clothes and food before we walk forty miles."

"Twenty."

Leslie rolled her eyes.

The harsh fact was they had to get far from Ambrose fast. But wet clothes could cause chafing and sores and infections. He sighed. "You're right. One day. We'll leave tomorrow."

"How are you going to find or trap enough food to feed us for six days in one day?"

"We can't carry everything. We'll ration what we have and find edibles on our way."

"We would need a whole summer's worth of berries to walk that far."

She was right. He glanced away. He'd tried to outsmart the Fellowship. Now they would starve. If something else didn't kill them first.

"You didn't hear Kenny last night, did you?"

He'd rested his eyes for a half-second last night and had fallen asleep. "No."

"He moaned and cried all night. His legs cramped." She shook her head. "He can't walk all day again today. I don't think I can either. My legs and feet hurt and I have blisters."

Blisters. Crap. Epically stupid to bring three kids out into the mountains without a tent or food or dry clothes. He hadn't planned for basics like blisters. No Band-Aids. No salves. No wool socks. No dry clothes.

Heck, Leslie was in a skirt. He glanced at her legs. Every inch bore scratches or scrapes. From his article to his stupidity, he had doomed them.

"We're safe here for a couple of days, aren't we?"

He didn't want to answer that. The Second Sphere hunted them. They might hunt them on horses or mules or use hounds. She had her brave face on. She would walk on if he insisted. They all would. And they would have more blisters and injuries and pain. And it would be his fault. He took a shaky breath. "Yeah. We're safe here. For a couple of days."

She smiled. It wasn't one of her best. "So, you'll set some traps and we'll make a fire ring?"

Ian opened his mouth to argue, but common sense won again. "I'll dig an extended Dakota fire hole."

She cocked her head.

"A below ground fire pit with a long smoke channel."

A fire pit inside the cave with the smoke diverted downhill would be a lot of work, but worth it. Their hunters would search for the smoke and give him and the others a chance to escape in the other direction.

She scanned the clear blue sky. "I'll hang the blankets and sleeping bags out to dry."

"Do you still have that empty peanut butter jar?"

"Yeah. Carry our trash, remem—" A pained expression flickered across her face.

He ignored the deepening gorge inside himself. "Squirrels love peanut butter." *It probably smells too human. I'll try some acorns, too.*

"I'll help you with the fire pit and channel. Travis and Kenny can hunt for some dry wood—there are dry leaves in the back of the cave and—" She eyed the wet ground and dripping trees. "There's got to be some dry wood somewhere—under a tree or something." Her voice quivered.

"I'll bet you could find some late-season berries or hickory nuts," Ian said. "Or persimmons—" A twig snapped behind them. Ian whirled toward the sound.

"Wild sugarplums? Yum!" Travis rubbed his stomach and joined them. "But this growing boy needs meat. I'm going to catch and roast a mountain trout."

Ian cocked his head. "Spearfishing, right?"

Travis grinned.

"That's a great idea." *Not easy, but it might work.* Ian pulled the hunting knife from his belt. "Let's find us a branch that can become a spear."

It didn't take long to find a straight branch, strip it, and sharpen one end. Ian left Travis in icy creek water to his knees, stabbing at elusive mountain trout.

Using the hatchet and the knife, it took most of the day for Ian and Leslie to dig the fire pit and a channel. He lined the pit and channel with rocks while Leslie and Kenny went out to hunt for firewood. He stepped back and admired his handiwork.

Travis crawled in with the homemade spear clutched in one hand and limped across the cave. Tremors shook him and his feet and legs were fiery red.

Ian's chest tightened. "You stayed in the water too long." He tore off his jacket and tucked it around Travis's legs. "You know better than that."

Racked with shivers and chattering teeth, Travis nodded.

Ian hurried outside. The quilts and sleeping bags hung on the rope strung between two trees. The quilts were dry. He wadded them in a sloppy roll, took them into the cave, and swaddled Travis in the quilts.

He slipped his jacket back on and sat back on his heels. *I need to be a better leader.*

Kenny dragged in a rucksack that held a dozen ripe sugarplums. Leslie followed with a stack of firewood. She fussed over Travis while Ian found the matches and built a roaring fire.

For lunch, they split a can of Vienna sausage amongst them and for dessert, they had three of the juicy purple-orange fruits each. It barely dulled Ian's hunger.

He grabbed the empty peanut butter jar and a canteen. "Come with me, Travis. We need to set some animal traps."

Travis shook his head. "I'd have caught that last fish if I hadn't been shivering. I'm warmed up now. I'm going to try again."

Ian opened his mouth to demand that Travis come with him, then changed his mind. He needed time to himself. "You should wait until tomorrow otherwise you'll risk—"

"I won't get hypothermia again. I'll stay on land."

"Be sure you do."

After Travis left, Ian pulled Leslie aside. "Check on him in ten minutes."

She nodded.

"If I'm not back by dawn, pack up and run. Go to Buena Vista."

Leslie's brows furrowed and she shook her head. "We need to stick together." She side-eyed Kenny who sat by the fire and played in the sandy dirt.

Ian sought and locked eyes with hers. "Promise me. Leave at sunset. Not a minute later. On the west side of Buena Vista is Glen Maury Park. I'll meet you at the south end of the park. On the bridge over the Maury. At sunset. Every night for four nights."

She swallowed. "And if we don't meet after four nights?"

"Save yourselves."

She put a hand on his arm. "Don't make me wait at the bridge."

He gave her a grim smile. "It's a precaution. I'll be back tonight." He left her standing with her hands pressed to her chest.

———

Warm in the sun, the late fall air was much cooler in the shade. He walked and scanned the ground for tracks or scat. In wet areas, mud oozed into the tracks and made it difficult to tell an animal had passed through.

Finally, he spotted tiny tufts of rabbit fur stuck in some wild rhododendron branch. A rabbit or rabbits had passed through the bush more than once. He notched each of three sticks. One notch rested in the other, held the sticks together in the shape of a four. Where the trail entered the bush, he jabbed the long stick into the ground and propped the empty peanut butter jar against it. A heavy rock balanced on the angle of the four would drop on any squirrel that tried to get the peanut butter. After that, he hunted for acorns. Whole ones were rare.

He searched for another trail. He couldn't focus. His situation demanded better decisions. His life depended on it and, more importantly, his brothers' and sister's lives.

He-haw.

He started. *Another mule? Please, be a hill person.* He steeled himself to peek.

Cock-a-doodle-do.

His pulse rate doubled.

A rooster? He peered through an opening in the trees.

Beyond the trees stretched a half-plowed field. In the unplowed half stood rows and rows of green stalks with shriveled and frost-blackened leaves. The mule, with its fire-ax-carrying old woman, stood next to a farmer-occupied tractor halfway down a plowed row. At the end of the field and to their right stood a red barn and a shed. Across from the barn sat a white farmhouse.

Ian spun and pressed his back against a bumpy tree trunk. Elbows glued to his sides, his lungs worked as if he'd raced that mule. The fact that he had never seen the farm before didn't surprise him. The mountains hid more secrets than the stars. But they also held far more people than he'd ever imagined—people who could report where he and Leslie and his brothers hid.

He peered around the trunk. The woman on the mule seemed friendly with the farmer. She pulled something out of her saddlebags and handed it to him. The farmer gave her a small sack. Hill people like her traded goods or bartered with everyone, including Fellowship members. She put the sack in her saddle-bag, waved goodbye to the farmer, and rode north, past the barn. Then she vanished into the trees and the tractor chugged to life and moved farther away.

Ian pulled back, leaned his head against the trunk, and forced himself to think. *I'm two miles or more from the cave. The house is on the other side of the field—two and a quarter miles, more or less. The cave will be safe for two or three days—if we're careful.*

His stomach burned and folded on itself.

The farm meant food, didn't it?

But the crops are already gone. And we can't buy a cow or a pig or even one tiny chick. But...Where there's a rooster, there are chickens... Ian's mouth watered at the memory of fried chicken. *Can't fry it—And still can't pay for it. Can't pay—could steal. Stealing eggs wouldn't be awful. Hens can always lay more eggs.*

He took one last look. The tractor continued plowing. No one else worked anywhere in the field or near the barn or the house. Ian made up his mind. He would be back after dark.

He left the way he came. Tree trunk to tree trunk. Until the forest swallowed all sounds and sights of him.

CHAPTER 9

WILLIAMS'S FINGERS hovered over the unopened folder on his makeshift desk in the sanctuary. His fingers curled; he couldn't make himself touch the Ambrose sleeper's folder.

Delaying the inevitable, he adjusted the burn of the mantle in the kerosene lamp. He brushed flakes of dried, peeling paint off his old-door-turned-desktop.

He shifted his weight in the pulpit chair with its too-straight back. *My appointment will walk through the door any minute. I must read this.* But his blood seethed and his stomach roiled against the idea of dealing with a sleeper again. He silently cursed his uncle and the Mitchell brothers.

The rich and influential Mitchell brothers met and worshiped the first Prophet. With their wealth and influence and powerful political friends, the Fellowship grew like wildflowers after a spring rain. But agnostics protested and plotted against them. Anxious to protect the Prophet, the Mitchell brothers funded and developed the Second Sphere. The Second Sphere kept the Prophet and the nation secure from the wars overseas and angry agnostics.

After Franklin D. Roosevelt was assassinated, the Mitchell brothers convinced President Garner to appoint the Prophet and the Fellowship Council as advisors for himself and his cabinet. The Second Sphere's responsibilities increased. As did the agnostics' attacks. But the agnostics defied every attempt to identify them. Until the older Mitchell brother established the sleepers. The sleepers identified and defeated countless dangerous dissidents.

Bile burned the back of Williams's throat. Despite knowing all that, he would never forget or forgive his uncle for the lies that caused his beloved aunt to commit suicide and forever shame Williams's family.

He breathed in for a five-count and released it over a slow five count. Two fingers pinched the corner of the file cover and opened it.

A sleeper for more than twenty years, Mr. Montgomery Jones Sr.'s file bulged with reports of suspicious anti-Fellowship activities. Williams paged past those.

He turned to the documents about Jones's son, Montgomery Jones, Jr. The best friend of Ian Hobart.

The younger Jones had filed hundreds of reports.

A cold draft stirred the papers, flickered the lamplight.

A shiver squirmed across Williams's shoulders and a certain sympathy for Hobart crept into his gut.

The crisp knock on the sanctuary door startled him.

He closed and flipped the folder over, smoothed his expression. "Enter."

Eighteen-year-old Montgomery Jones Jr. swept into the room and snapped a smart salute.

Williams returned the salute and studied the young man.

Five feet, ten inches tall, sturdy but not heavy, Jones had good bearing and neatly trimmed light brown hair. He wore a school letter jacket over a crisp blue shirt, a pair of jeans, and too much Aqua Velva. It struck Williams that the boy could have been his own son's school chum.

"At ease, Montgomery." Williams rose, gestured toward a pair of pews near one of the intact stained-glass windows. He sat first. "Sit. We're just going to chat for a while."

The boy's glance took in the makeshift office. He sat stiffly in the other pew and faced Williams. "Sir, please call me Monty. Montgomery is what my parents call me when I'm in trouble." He had a disarming smile.

Williams chuckled. "I know what that's like. Would you like something to drink?"

"No, thank you, sir. I'm fine."

"I've got some questions about your friend, Ian Hobart."

Not an eye blink or flicker crossed Monty's face. "What questions, sir?"

Williams pretended to relax, draped an arm across the back of the pew. "Tell me about him."

"I've known him all my life. I could tell you about things we did that made our moms mad or how we skipped school once, but I don't think that's what you're asking for. What is it you want to know?"

Williams gritted his teeth and ignored the increased burn at the back of his throat. How smooth Monty's answer was—at the age of eighteen he was already a consummate equivocator. He'd underestimated this kid. "Do you know where he is?"

"No, sir."

Not a single twitch. *Not a lie.* "When did you last see him?"

"Um," Monty glanced down and to the left. "At the paper, sir, on um, Friday afternoon."

Ah, he's good but that's a lie. "If he had to hide, where do you think he'd go?"

Monty squared himself, looked Williams in the eye. "Golly sir, he'd go to the mountains, to his father's hunting cabin."

"I see." Williams stretched his legs out. Monty hadn't given him anything not in the reports. "Did he go to this cabin often?"

"Every year he and his father take four hunting trips. The whole family goes a couple more times."

He didn't react to the verb tense. "How often did you go with them?"

"I've been once or twice." The boy leaned back. The pew creaked.

"Are there any weapons kept at the cabin?"

"Not that I know of, sir."

He hasn't asked about his friend. He's hiding something. Williams rose, picked the file up off his desk. "This file says you were the source of many of the reports about the Hobart family's anti-Fellowship activities. Is that true?"

"Yes, sir. I value friendships but not at the price of my loyalty to the Fellowship."

"And you have no idea where your friend is right now?"

"None, sir." Monty's expression showed no concern.

He's developed a solid poker face. A liar's liar.

Maybe he values his friendship more than he's admitted. Not uncommon for a young man. "Do you think you could take me to his family's hunting cabin?"

"Yes, sir. When would you like to go?"

"Now." Williams crossed to the door.

"Sir..." Monty held the door partly open. "May I suggest you change into something more casual? There's no road where we're going."

"You let me worry about my wardrobe." Williams strode out of the sanctuary. Adler already had the car waiting by the door.

———

Two hours later, he tromped through naked elms and oaks and old pines. His pant legs were covered in pollen and sticky leaves and sharp burrs. Mud and fallen leaves caked his shoes. He suspected Monty had taken him on a longer-than-necessary route.

Monty enthusiastically identified plants and birds and told tales of hunting with Ian. An ambitious young man, his stories often demonstrated how useful he was to the Second Sphere.

Williams followed Monty through a stand of pines so thick that a false darkness fell. The stink of damp earth and dead things burned inside his nose in that going-to-sneeze-not-going-to-sneeze way. He pinched his nostrils until the burn abated.

Monty stopped. Beyond him, squeezed tight between the pines stood a tiny log cabin. Williams couldn't tell whether the pines grew so close by design or neglect.

Dark and silent, the cabin appeared unoccupied. He unsnapped the retention strap of his holster and sidled up between the lone window and the door.

A quick peek in the window revealed a vacant and dark interior. He tried the door. It opened noiselessly.

A quick walk-through confirmed the Hobarts weren't here.

He returned to the main room. Smooth varnished wood shelves hung above a floating kitchen counter with more shelves below it. He picked up a cooking pot—dust lay inside it. His fingers detected no heat from the cold, black potbellied stove that stood in the north corner. The ash clean-out door squeaked when he opened it and peered at the clean ash pan.

A curtain concealed the back half of the cabin. He moved it and dust showered down on him. He sneezed, twice. More curtains divided that space into three separate sleeping areas and added to the dust in the air. The bare mattresses showed no sign of recent occupancy. He didn't pat the mattress for fear of more dust.

A single cupboard in the back opened without difficulty. It held neatly stacked linens. No clothes. No weapons. No sign of the Hobarts.

Williams stepped outside. Monty followed and stood silently while Williams scanned the woods around them.

From what Monty had said, the Hobart children had the skills to survive in the wild.

Even if he summoned every Cleaner under his command and they scoured this place for weeks, it was unlikely that they'd find Hobart and his siblings.

The area was too large, the forest too dense, and the land too rugged.

The entire army of hounds specially trained for the Second Sphere might not ever find the children. Then again, the dogs might. He'd seen dogs find runners that humans couldn't. Hounds were not a budget item for Cleaners but, he had a favor he might call in....

He turned to Monty. "There are no other cabins or places where you would expect your friend to hide?"

Monty's eyes met his without a moment's hesitation. "Sir, I'd tell you if I knew where Ian is. I don't."

He smiled at Monty like the vile sleeper had been useful. "I appreciate your help, young man." *I know you've lied about something, but I'm not going to get anything else out of you today.* At least not by the direct approach. "Of course, you'll let me know if your friend contacts you in any way?"

"Of course."

CHAPTER 10

THE COALS in the fire pit glowed red-hot but it didn't warm Ian. Today's discoveries and decisions sat like an icy lump in his middle. He tried to ignore it and eat his dinner.

Seated Indian-style next to him, Leslie stared into the fire. Travis and Kenny had finished first and had gone out to gather more firewood before it got too dark.

He chewed his last bit of Spam. Washed it down with weak sassafras tea in a handmade aluminum foil cup that leaked.

"I was stupid."

Leslie's comment penetrated his hundredth mental replay of the farm's layout. "Huh?"

"In the kitchen—I should have grabbed meat. All the meat." She fed the fire a portion of a thick limb. Flames licked around the fresh log.

"You did okay."

"That Spam was the last can of meat."

"What do you mean? The bag's half full."

"There's one can of chili and one of pork and beans. The rest are green beans, peas, corn..." She bit her lower lip.

"I should have rationed the meat."

Her glare nailed him. "*We* should have."

He decided not to argue the point and patted her arm awkwardly. "You did good, Les."

That didn't help. Her frown and the furrows in her forehead deepened. *Leslie can't give up. She never gives up.*

He raised his aluminum foil cup, shaped from foil she stole from the house. It dribbled warm sassafras-flavored water on his leg. "You did better than me. I didn't think about food." He had been preoccupied with getting away from the Second Sphere. Food and clothes and all the things they needed to be safe—not on his mind at all.

"What are we going to do?" She picked up a twig, broke off a tiny bit, and threw it in the fire.

"We survive." He hunched his shoulders, wrapped one hand over the other fist, and told her about the farm.

Understanding then horror lit her face. "You're going to steal from the farm?"

"You got any better ideas?"

The fire crackled.

Snap. A piece of twig flew into the fire. Another then another followed. She watched them turn to ash. "We don't have many options, do we?" The last piece of the twig vanished in the flames. "You shouldn't go alone. I'll go with you."

"No, it's better if you stay here." Bad enough that he'd be a thief. "That way, if I don't come back—"

"If you—what?" She gaped at him.

"—if I don't come back before dawn, you tknow what to do."

"Go to Buena Vista? What if you are only five minutes late? I won't leave you behind." She blinked and blinked and blinked.

"I plan to be here before dawn. But we have to be adults about this and have a plan in case it takes longer than I expect." *Or I get arrested or shot dead.* He banished that thought, concentrated on projecting calm confidence. "If I'm late, I'll meet you on the Maury River Road bridge. If I'm not there after four nights,

I'm not coming. Do whatever you can to save yourself and the boys."

She held his gaze. "That's just a precaution right?"

"That's all. A precaution."

"Promise, you'll come back with or without food."

"I'll get us some food *and* I'll be back, Leslie. I promise." He slung a canteen and empty rucksack over his shoulder, prayed he hadn't lied, and left his siblings behind.

———

Ian peered through the trees at the moonlit field and the farm brightly lit by an outdoor light that stood between him and the barn and the house. His chest tingled like a tuning fork had been struck inside him.

If he repositioned and approached from behind the barn, he had twice the distance to cross in a bright and open field. From here the distance was less, but the dark windows of the house watched him.

If Leslie were here, she would say go home empty-handed.

He wasn't Leslie. He shook his hands out.

I can do this. I will do this. I have to do this.

He crouched and sped across the freshly plowed field. The empty rucksack on his back flapped like broken wings.

Eyes on the house, he ran to the barn, flattened himself against the back wall. Ragged gasps fed him air but didn't stop his breathlessness.

He listened. His heart beat louder than the crickets that resumed their chorus. No alarms. No shouts. He blew out a breath and peered around the corner of the barn.

The well-lit ground between the barn and the house remained vacant. From this angle, a faint light flickered deep inside the house. Beside the house, a pale-yellow 1952 Mercury sat in the drive. The drive ran from the side of the house downhill toward Route 130.

Ian slid across to the other side of the barn. The henhouse, a shed with a wire-enclosed run, stood in the shadow of the barn. Dark and shut tight. He crept through the shadow, out of sight of the house.

The simple gate latch lifted easily. He stepped inside. Instead of a room full of chickens, he stood in a closet-sized storage room with one interior door. Stacks of stuff filled the tiny space—boxes of plastic shoe covers, bags of chicken feed, stacks of large plastic bowls, and a stack of egg cartons.

His hands shook but he took the top two cartons. At least now he wouldn't have to transport fragile eggs in the empty rucksack he carried. He lifted the hook on the interior door.

Inside the henhouse dark, warm, humid air with a faint acrid ammonia odor blanketed him. Moonlight filtered through ventilation windows high on the walls. A spooky, lumpy shadow lined one wall.

His eyes adjusted to the dim light. The lumpy shape resolved. Dozens of chickens roosted on horizontal boards that stair-stepped up the wall.

The opposite wall held small boxes closed with chicken wire doors, triple-stacked. He'd expected their nests to be in the open.

The birds purred and clucked and squawked and watched him. They gave him the willies.

They're used to people taking their eggs. I can just reach in and take the eggs...

He took a step. The birds stirred, clucked and squawked louder. He froze. Waited to be caught. Certain the farmer would hear the muttering hens and his panic-driven heart. The hens settled down. His heart didn't.

Bit by bit he eased his weight from one foot to the other. It took an age to creep to the first straw-lined box. It held an empty nest. The next three were also empty.

In the fifth box, a hen sat on the nest. He raised the chicken wire door, slid his trembly hand under her. She squawked softly. He pulled out an egg and beamed at the warm, speckled egg he put into the carton. His pulse slowed from a speeding sports car to a speeding station wagon.

The next nest held another hen. She pecked his hand. He snapped his lips together and held in a yelp. Somehow he still managed to pull an egg out from under her.

He crept down the line of nests. Fifteen eggs. More than he needed, in case he'd taken a fertilized egg or two.

The outer door of the hen house creaked. Ian's pulse leaped into overdrive. His gaze bounced around the hen house. No place to hide.

The latch on the interior door rattled. Light blazed around him.

"What do ya think yer doing—" The man's voice was calm. "—contaminatin' my hen house and stealin' from my hens?"

Breathing hard, he turned to face the man. A flashlight blinded him. He shielded his eyes with one hand and focused on the shotgun aimed at him. His heart tried to beat the bullet, tried to burst out of his ribs.

The farmer lowered the light. "Boy, why d'ya come a-stealing?"

Dry swallows didn't help.

Tall and lean and grizzled, the old man wore a tan jacket over a pair of striped flannel pajamas.

Ian quivered with run-away-run-away-run-away-now energy. He couldn't stop staring down the double barrels of the shotgun.

"Do ya know anythin' about honor, boy?" His light traveled up and down Ian. "Honorable men don't come a-stealing."

He's gonna shoot me or call the police. Ian didn't know which was worse.

"Ya best understand another thing. Them thieves get caught —those Fellowship folk don't take kindly to." The farmer's droll tone chilled Ian. "They send ya to one of them re-education centers. Re-education my ass." He bent as if to spit, swallowed it. "Be nothin' but brainwash an' torture." The light settled on the egg cartons Ian held.

"Ya ain't alone out there, are ya?"

He didn't answer.

"Now there be some honorable men who altercate with the Fellowship. Are ya one o' them?"

The farmer closed in a couple of steps. Lowered his shotgun.

Ian darted toward the old man, reached him before he raised the shotgun. He shoved the farmer with all his might and ran.

Something banged against the floor behind him.

He didn't pause, didn't look back.

"Dad-gum-it." the farmer shouted. "I's just gonna give ya more eggs."

Right. Ian surged around the barn, then sped across the field, and into the trees in the opposite direction of the cave.

The moon was a spotlight he wished he could break with a well-aimed rock.

He ran until he couldn't breathe anymore. He stopped, bent, and gasped for breath.

No sounds of pursuit, no barking, no shouting followed him. Tremors shook him, weakened his knees. He sank to the ground, head bowed.

An owl hooted, startled him. He spun around fast. Then again, slower. No pursuers approached. *Can't stay here. Can't go back to the cave. Not yet.* He took off at a trot.

The cold night air made his footsteps unnaturally loud. Fast or quiet. He chose fast.

Stupid old man's lecture about Redemption saved me.

He no longer feared Redemption. Wanted by the Second Sphere and now a thief, Redemption wasn't his fate. He'd be Taken or tried and executed.

I had no choice. They took Ma, Pop, and Junior. They forced me to become a thief.

His trot gave way to a jog then faded to a dogged plod. A cramp seized his hand. He switched the egg cartons to the other hand.

The night air grew colder chilled him through his sweat-soaked clothes. But it was more than the air that sent the chill deep into his bones.

Eventually, the Second Sphere would catch him. But he wouldn't make it easy.

CHAPTER 11

A CHILLY DRAFT blew through broken stained-glass windows and holes in the brick walls of the sanctuary. Williams pressed the Handie Talkie to his ear with frozen fingers and listened to the ultra-calm voice of Major Banks. *My days are numbered.* He could tell by the detached way the Major had just given him all the statistics for his past successes.

"Four children have beaten you and your whole team for four days. It's astonishing and sad."

Maybe his hours were numbered.

"Sir, I have a plan in the works. I need two or three more days."

"Am I supposed to believe that the next three days will be more successful than the past four days? What has changed since yesterday? Where is it mentioned in your report?"

Williams loosened his tie. "New information came in last night. We're working to verify it. Give me seventy-two hours. I'll bring the children in." During his surveillance, Nickerson had observed Monty using a Handie Talkie. The parabolic microphone picked up him calling for the oldest boy.

"I've always liked you, Williams. Therefore, I'm flying in tomorrow to assess the situation." Static. Silence. He'd disconnected. Worse, if it had been a telephone, the receiver had been slammed down.

Waves of cold and hot washed over Williams. He listened to the static long enough to be certain he didn't "accidentally" hang up on the boss.

He turned off the Handie Talkie, placed it in its cradle and stared through it.

Every time the Major "visited" an operation, the crew was reassigned or simply disappeared. Williams's pulse beat steady and hard and loud. *I hope the Azrael assigned to me use a bullet. A garrote is--messy.*

But I'm not going to wait for her to come. Time to put some pressure on young Monty. "Adler."

Adler's shoes clacked across the foyer floor, then he appeared in the doorway. "Yes, sir?" His uniform somehow clean and crisp in this God-forsaken place.

Williams straightened his tie, brushed red brick dust off his thighs, and gave himself a mental shake. *I am still in charge here no matter how disheveled my clothes.* "Bring that boy, Monty, here. Thirty minutes."

"Yes, sir."

He paced and wished he were in his infinitely more comfortable office in the District.

Exactly thirty minutes later, Monty strode into the room with cocky confidence. He came to attention and saluted, his smile unwavering.

Williams took note of the smug smile. *Perhaps Monty believes he has a protector. If he does, I'm about to stick the final seal on my death warrant.* He forced himself to relax "Have you heard from Hobart?"

"Not yet, sir."

"You said you know this boy."

Monty's expression grew wary. "I do, sir. He'll contact me—"

"Are you certain he hasn't called you on that Handie Talkie you keep in your bedroom?"

Monty stilled, his stance stiffened. "Sir, he has not contacted me. He will—in a day or two, likely after dark."

Williams rose and crowded into Monty's personal space. "I don't like people who obfuscate."

Monty continued to stare straight ahead, straight at Williams's chin. "What would you have me do, sir?"

"You will contact Hobart. Convince him that you are in danger because you helped him escape. You need him."

He tilted his head back and smiled his charming boy smile. His pupils dilated. "That's a good plan sir, as soon as Ian reaches out—"

"Not soon enough." *A liar can't control his pupils.* Williams kept his voice level. "You will arrange a meet this evening, tomorrow evening at the latest."

Monty's eyes darted left of Williams's shoulder. He blinked, refocused, and locked eyes with Williams. "Yes, sir. Where do you want us to meet?"

He turned his back on Monty, noted that Adler stood behind him. He crossed to stare out a window. Even the stained glass couldn't brighten the gray sky and the bare trees. "It must be an area we can control but where he will feel safe, a public place."

"A public place?" Monty pursed his lips and tilted his head. "Like a public park?"

Williams folded his arms across his chest and turned a stony face to the boy.

"Too big and too public," Adler explained to Monty. "Here perhaps?"

Monty gave him a how-dumb-can-you-be look.

Adler quirked his mouth. "Movie theater?"

"Dark, limited space—" Williams considered the possibilities.

"We can have our men sitting inside before he arrives. Barricade the back door and we have limited exits to cover."

Monty shook his head. "No. Ian's not stupid enough to fall for that. Those limitations will be in his mind, too. I won't get him to agree to meet anywhere like that."

"And where is it that you think he'd agree to meet?"

"A tree house." Monty described its location.

Williams glanced an order at Adler.

A quick trip to the foyer and Adler returned with a geological survey map and spread it open on Williams's desk. The paper crinkled and lifted in the draft. Alder anchored it with the kerosene lamp on one corner and a discarded hymnal he plucked from the floor on the other.

Monty pointed to a location on the Northwest side of Ambrose. "But if you surround the place, Ian won't come."

Williams frowned and studied the map. It was isolated but difficult to surround with four men. "And you can lure all four of them to this tree house?"

His eyes widened. "No, sir. The tree house is a place for the two of us." His face relaxed into its usual neutral expression. "I was supposed to meet with Ian, you would capture him, then learn the location of the others. Has the plan changed, sir?"

Williams tapped the map with his index finger three times. His taps turned the paper map into a tiny snare drum. *When a strong leader is faced with a crisis, he changes tactics, not strategy.* "Just exploring the possibilities, young man." He folded his hands together and leaned forward. "The plan—to capture Hobart—is the same. The timeline isn't."

This time Monty held his composure. "And what is the timeline now, sir?"

Young Monty has balls. "Meet him tonight, tomorrow night at the latest." He gave Monty a pointed glare. "You're against the clock."

"Yes, sir." Monty's expression didn't change.

A sense of foreboding filled him. That was confidence, not false bravado. He spun on his heel, the clack of his footsteps more sure and solid than his insides. He stopped at the other end of the sanctuary. Recovered his equilibrium. Turned and waved Monty away. "Dismissed."

Monty turned on his heel and strode out of the room.

Williams glared at Adler who hadn't moved.

"Sir, it might be better if we wait for Hobart to contact Monty on his own terms."

"It won't be better if we're dead." His voice was harsh, like the reality.

Adler stood a tiny bit straighter. "Yes, sir."

"Who's taking him home?"

"Nickerson, sir."

Williams waved a dismissal at Adler and returned to his desk. But Adler didn't leave. "Was there something else?"

"The farmer supplying the Big Island unit reports that a fox stole two dozen eggs."

"Why are you telling me this? Foxes steal eggs—"

"They don't wear tennis shoes."

A slow smile spread across Williams' face. "We might have a chance after all. Adler, get my car."

CHAPTER 12

THE AROMA of eggs cooking drifted into Ian's dream. *Ma fixed breakfast.*

He rolled over; a hand flopped onto a rock. "Ow!" Awake, memory returned like a punch in the gut. *Ma's gone. I stole from the farm.* He sat up, rubbed his hand.

"Hello, sleepyhead," Leslie said. "Hungry?" She crouched down next to him and offered a wad of ash-smudged aluminum foil she held with leaves as pot holders. "Be careful, it's hot."

He peeled the foil back. Inside the double layer of aluminum foil laid perfectly scrambled eggs. Hot, melt-in-your-mouth eggs warmed him from his mouth all the way down to his stomach. He tipped the last of the eggs into his mouth, turned the foil inside out, and licked it clean.

Leslie sat across from him. Elbows on her knees, chin on her fists, she studied him.

"That was great. Did you eat?"

"Hours ago."

He glanced around the empty cave. "Where are Kenny and Travis?" With the uneven light from the fire, he couldn't be sure they weren't in the dark corners.

"I sent them to find berries, or nuts, or more persimmons."

"Good." He stretched. "What time of day is it?"

She smiled. "It'll be dusk soon."

"I've slept all day?"

"You mumbled a lot in your sleep. Did you have nightmares?"

"Mumbled?" The escape ghosted through his memory. "Did I say anything—important?"

"You said no—a lot. And—" She scrunched her face up and peered at him. "Did you get caught?"

For a second Ian considered telling her the truth, but it would just worry her more. "Nah. It went okay, but I don't think I should go back there." He gave a half-snort, half-laugh. "I didn't know, but apparently hens don't lay eggs at night. "

"Are you sorry you did it?" She studied his face intently.

He considered his answer. "No. We had to eat. But we'll need a lot more food. We've got to figure something else out."

Leslie fidgeted. She had something on her mind. "I think, if we're going to be here for a while, we need heavy clothes and lanterns and—tons of stuff. We should ask Mrs. Miller. She would be glad to help us."

Ian stiffened. There was no way he'd ever ask their former neighbor, Mrs. Miller, for anything. "No." He tried and failed to control the blush that rose to his cheeks.

Leslie straightened and gaped at him as if he had spoken in Latin. "She could get us blankets and—"

"It's too dangerous." He couldn't meet Leslie's eyes. He would have called Mrs. Miller nice once, too. She had always paid attention to him, flattered him, and he'd fallen for her—hard. *But to her, I was nothing but a stupid kid.*

He'd been cleaning gutters for Pop when he happened to glance at the Miller's house. Mrs. Miller stood near the bedroom window. She wore a—he wasn't certain what to call it besides red and take-his-breath-away-sexy.

The silky fabric curved around her breasts and waist. Strings around her neck and back kept it on. It was not a Fellowship-approved outfit. But Ian couldn't get that image out of his mind.

"Okay, smartie. It would be dangerous, but how do you plan to keep us from starving or freezing to death?" Leslie's voice jerked him back to now.

"Stealing one meal at a time isn't a good long-term plan."

Leslie snorted.

"I need to rob a store with lots of food. That way, one robbery gives us a week of meals."

"You mean you want to rob a grocery or supermarket?"

"No. Big supermarkets will have those new security cameras. What we need are small, isolated shops. Like the camp stores or Stop-and-Go's. I can scout them during the day. Break-in at night. Take what we need."

"Those are owned by folks like Ma and Pop."

"I'll do as little damage as I can."

He didn't like it, but Leslie's frown registered downright disapproval.

"I know—" he said. "I'll rob stores that display the shield. Like Robin Hood. I'll steal from the Fellowship. Give to the poor —the Hobarts."

Leslie laughed.

Heat rose to Ian's face. Mrs. Miller had laughed at him, too. He tried to tell her he loved her at one of their weekend barbecues. She announced to everyone what a silly, lovesick boy he was, and laughed—loud. "Don't laugh." He glowered at the fire.

Leslie covered her mouth. "I'm sorry." Her voice still held a smile.

Ian glared at her. "It's not like we can buy what we need."

"I know." She scanned the cave. Her gaze lingered on the pine straw beds where Travis and Kenny slept. "I will do whatever it takes. Travis and Kenny have to survive. I won't let the

Fellowship erase the whole Hobart family." She faced him. "We'll be Robin Hoods together. I'll be your lookout."

Ian drew back, startled. He hadn't thought of that, but his gut said Leslie shouldn't be the lookout. He shook his head. "I don't think we should leave Kenny alone."

"He'd be with Travis."

"He does better with you." Then it hit Ian. It *would* be worse if Leslie got caught instead of him. "Your work experience will lead to a good job. One that pays real money."

Her face clouded. "But I can't work in a doctor's office—" Her face cleared. "But I could work at a veterinarian's office like Junior—or a pharmacy." She shook her head. "I can't give my references—oh—but I can show them I know what I'm doing, can't I? And you—can't be a reporter—cover the news, go to court, or city council meetings—sooner or later a Fellowship member would recognize you—" She touched his arm. "What will you do?"

He straightened, shook off her hand. "Don't worry about me. I'll be a store clerk or something." *Something like join the rebels. Fight the Fellowship.*

"Okay. Travis will be your lookout. When do you think—?"

"Tomorrow night." He didn't have to like it, but growing boys —Travis and Kenny—needed protein.

"Two thefts in this area in a couple of days—they'll figure it's us."

"Yeah." His already hollow insides hollowed out more.

"We'll pack in the morning. Kenny and I will cover up the fire pit and trough, erase all signs we were here."

"If it gets to be dawn and we're not back—"

She swallowed. "Kenny and I will head for Buena Vista. If you—if you don't catch up—we'll—wait at the Maury River bridge at sunset every day for a week." Her look dared him to argue.

He held her gaze. "We'll be there, Les." She needed the promise. He'd try to keep it. But someday he wouldn't.

CHAPTER 13

CROUCHED BEHIND A RAISED RAILROAD BED, Ian watched Dixie's Gas and Food Mart across the street. The well-lit storefront and awning over the three gas pumps blazed in the night.

Next to him, Travis peered over the tracks and bounced on his toes. "How much longer?"

"Two hours. They don't close until nine."

"Ugh." Travis turned and sat with his back to the railroad berm.

A cream-colored Mercury Monterey sat at the pumps and two more cars parked alongside the store. The drivers shopped inside.

"Why did we come two hours early?"

"It was a good idea at the time." Ian didn't blame him for asking, the empty rucksack on his back billowed and popped in the damp, chilly wind, his fingers were frozen, and the creepy-crawlies ran up and down his back. He snugged the hood of his coat down around his face and buried his fists in the pockets. It didn't help.

An impenetrable-looking rectangle of concrete block painted white, the Food Mart had a flat roof with a triangular extension above the door. Tall, aluminum framed windows wrapped around a single rounded corner to the glass and aluminum front door. A large sticker in the door's glass proclaimed the place Fellowship Member Owned. Large windows lined the other side of the front wall to the next corner.

Ian's heart chided him—stu-pid, stu-pid, stu-pid. He focused on the Fellowship sticker. Focused on becoming a Robin Hood.

Visible through the front window, a tall, skinny woman with a head of unruly brown curls, stood behind the cash register and faced the door. The cashier greeted every customer. Ian prayed that the owners wouldn't blame her.

A four-door Oldsmobile drove up. A man and woman exited the car and entered the Food Mart. They disappeared into the store then reappeared and stood at the counter.

The cashier smiled and chatted and rang up their purchases.

The man and woman each carried a full paper sack to their car and pulled back onto the highway.

Ding-Ding. Ding-Ding. An aqua-colored Bel Air convertible with its top up stopped at the gas pump.

A young man in a gray jumpsuit came out of the store. He spoke to the driver, fueled the car, and cleaned the front window. The car drove off and the young man disappeared back inside.

In endless numbers, cars and customers came and went. From time to time the attendant would appear, say something to the cashier or service another vehicle, then fade into the back of the store. So many bags of groceries left the shop that Ian wondered if there'd be anything left worth stealing.

The evening wore on and the store had fewer and fewer customers.

Overhead clouds obscured the moon. The air transformed into a frosty mist. Ian shivered and pulled his thin jacket close around his neck.

The attendant appeared and flipped the open sign to closed.

He waved goodbye to the cashier, hurried to his car, and drove away.

Energy surged through Ian. Almost time. Almost time to turn into Robin Hood.

Thirty minutes later, most of the interior lights and all the exterior lights went out. The cashier closed and locked the door behind her and then she was gone.

Ian's pulse jumped and his muscles twitched. He concentrated on the plan. The single streetlight near Dixie's was at the far corner of the property. If Travis hid under the awning and behind the pump, he would be invisible.

Travis got his feet underneath him, ready to stand.

Ian put a hand on Travis's shoulder, held him down. "We don't want a late customer or a cleaning service to find us inside."

Travis expelled a big, noisy breath, but settled back down to wait.

Fewer and fewer cars passed the store.

The crickets fell silent.

A car whined past in the distance.

Ian checked his watch. By now most people were home, watching TV, or getting ready for bed. His pulse still thumped, but his breathing steadied.

"Remember what you're supposed to do, Travis?"

"Hide behind one of the pumps and keep watch."

"Right. When I'm ready to leave I'll signal three times with the flashlight. What else?"

Travis rolled his eyes and recited in a sing-song, "I holler if anyone comes. I don't wait. I run straight behind the building and into the woods. You'll be right behind me. But it'd be faster—"

"We talked about this. You hold up your end. Our lives depend on it." A shudder rippled through Ian at his father's words coming out of his mouth.

His younger brother quirked his mouth but nodded.

"Promise me."

"Cross my heart."

Ian stared at his brother, the brother he was about to turn into a thief. Any minute his quivering heart and lungs would burst. He tried to ignore them, tried to project calm to Travis, tried to think like Robin Hood. He squared his shoulders. "Let's go."

They darted across the street.

Travis positioned himself behind the center pump.

Ian picked up a can of oil from the tiered display in front of the window and threw the can at the door.

Glass exploded, then rained on the floor. The oilcan landed with a metallic *thunk* and rolled partway down the aisle. He reached inside, unlocked the door.

A glance back at Travis revealed his little brother was doing exactly what he was supposed to.

Ian entered the store and searched for a pair of gloves.

There weren't any.

They don't have my fingerprints. Maybe they won't figure out who I am.

His stomach twisted and growled at the sight of so much food. He pushed forward and grabbed all the hot dogs they had in the refrigerator case.

He took all four cans of spam on the shelf and then stared at all the rest of the canned goods. The spam had a key for opening the can. Other canned goods presented a problem but he wasn't going to leave good food behind—he'd open the cans with the knife or the axe. He scooped all the cans of chili and the cans of pork and beans off the shelf and into his rucksack. A tiny butterfly can opener hung on a display card at the end of the canned goods aisle. He grinned and grabbed it.

Around the next corner, he seized canned milk, three boxes of powdered milk, and four boxes of Cheerios. A laugh burst from his lips. He couldn't wait to show Leslie all this food.

He took cans of tuna and soup and snatched several boxes of matches and the six cans of Sterno that sat on the shelf. Next, he paused at the ice cream. He wished he had some way to take it back to camp. But it would melt before he got there.

In the back corner of the store, a wall display held a small selection of coats. Ian couldn't believe it. Large, weatherproof, warm coats. He tried one on. Large for him, but that was okay. He zipped it halfway up and stuffed a small jacket inside his new jacket then tied two medium-sized ones around his waist. There were gloves, too. He jammed four pairs, into his pockets.

Around the next corner, a four-foot-tall stack of Twinkie boxes brought him to a halt.

His mouth watered. His rucksack was already too heavy but after what they'd been through, they deserved some sweets. He couldn't pass them up—he took two boxes.

The sides and top of the rucksack bulged. He couldn't close it up. He pulled the drawstring tight around the exposed Twinkie boxes and hoisted the thing over his shoulder. Despite the padding in his jacket, the straps dug into his skin.

He pointed the flashlight at the front window, turned it on and off three times in quick succession.

The storeroom was tiny and crowded with boxes and shelves. He trotted past them, unlocked the back door, then pulled it shut behind him. He turned. Travis waited for him at the bottom of the steps.

Ian staggered down the steps. The food was heavier than he'd estimated. He untied one of the coats from around his waist and handed it to Travis. "Merry Christmas—sort of."

Travis gaped and grinned and slipped it on. "Thanks."

They ran across the back yard into the trees. After two minutes, Ian had to put the sack down and rest. The top of the rucksack gaped open. The Twinkie boxes were missing. "Darn it."

"What?" Travis asked.

"The Twinkies must have fallen out back there."

"Twinkies?" Even in the dark, Travis's face lit up. "I'll get them."

"No, it's not worth—"

But Travis had already raced back toward the store.

Ian hurried after him, slower—pacing himself because of the weight of the rucksack.

"No!" Travis screamed.

Ian glimpsed Travis through the trees. His heart twisted and stuttered. He couldn't breathe.

Travis struggled against a man who dragged him toward a Sheriff's Deputy car parked on one side of the building.

A light swept the tree line a foot from where Ian stood. A second deputy searched the back yard. Still, Ian took an involuntary step toward Travis.

"Hey—There's another one," a voice called. "I'm in pursuit."

Ian turned and ran the other direction. *I'll find you, Travis. Don't give up. I'll find you.*

CHAPTER 14

THE INCESSANT RINGING WOKE WILLIAMS. He slapped the alarm clock but the ringing continued. *Oh, the phone.* "Hello?"

"Sorry to disturb you, sir," Adler's voice didn't sound sorry. "I thought you'd want to know."

Williams rubbed his face with his free hand and peered at the clock. Midnight. "Now what?"

"We have a lead."

Electricity shot through him. He sat bolt upright. "On our targets?"

"Yes, sir. A robbery. I'll have the car waiting for you at the front door."

———

At one AM, Williams stood in the near-freezing temperatures behind Dixie's Food and Gas Mart. He jammed his frozen fingers deep into his trench coat pockets and glared at the tennis shoeprint in the damp forest floor. *It has to be the oldest Hobart boy's.*

The deputies had declined to fingerprint the store. Williams couldn't blame them. Dixie's averaged three hundred customers a week, many of them out-of-towners. Besides, Hobart's finger-prints weren't on file. He turned to Adler. "How long ago did you say this happened?"

"One and a quarter hours ago."

"They caught the middle boy? Where is he?"

"In a holding cell at the Sheriff's office in Lynchburg."

Williams's hand rasped against the stubble on his chin. That meant the middle boy had spent a couple of hours worried about what would happen to him. The perfect set-up to loosen his tongue. "Instruct the Sheriff's office that no one, and I mean no one, is to interrogate young Hobart. Wake Nickerson. Have him pick the boy up and take him to the church. Lock him up —somewhere."

"There's a storage closet on the north side of the pulpit."

"Perfect."

"Should we pursue the older boy, sir?"

"We will but first I have a call to make." He didn't know how good the scent would be but at least he had something.

An hour later, a black, older model Ford pickup pulled into the parking lot. On the vehicle's door, a hound's portrait sat in an orange shield emblazoned with the words James River Blood-hounds. The words and the shield fluoresced in the streetlight.

Fischer unfolded out of the vehicle. At six-eleven, he was a foot taller than Williams. "Good to see you, Willy." He was the only person who got away with calling Williams that stupid name.

Williams shook his hand. "I appreciate your help." *Someday Fischer will consider his debt for saving his family repaid.*

"How could I refuse? By-the-by, Audrey and the kids say hi— and you want me to finish the pleasantries and get to work, yes?"

Williams relaxed his tense muscles and his frown. "Yes. One man entered the store after the juveniles. But I've kept everyone else out. Tell me your dog can get a scent."

"In a store where many people come, Willy?" Fischer lowered his tailgate. "You know Xena must have a specific scent to seek." A wuff and snuffle greeted him.

"One of them used a can to break the door glass." Williams held up a hand to stop Fischer's protest. "Adler cleaned up the glass to protect your pooch."

"I see. We will hope the can holds enough scent." Fischer opened one of the large dog carriers. "Come, Xena." A large brown and black dog with long, droopy ears leaped to the ground.

"A piece of clothing would be better, of course." Fischer put a harness and long leash on the dog then knelt at the dog's side, rubbed her chest, neck, and head vigorously. "Are you ready, girl? Ready to work?" Her tail went up and waved back and forth. "That's a girl. Let's get to work. Xena, work."

Williams led them through the door to where the dented oil can lay.

Fischer pointed to the can. "Xena, smell." The dog probed the can with her nose and a loud snuffle-sniff. "Xena, seek!"

The dog put her nose to the ground and zigzagged down the aisle. She surged down the next aisle, then out the open back door, across the pavement, and into the trees.

Williams tamped his soaring expectations down and trotted to keep Fischer and the dog in sight. She followed an invisible trail for forty-five minutes.

And then she stopped to smell a thicket of Mountain Laurel over and over. Williams chewed the inside of his cheek and silently urged the dog to move faster while she sniffed the ground in an ever-widening area.

She stopped, looked at Fischer and whined.

"What's she doing?"

"She's lost the scent."

Blast! If the dog lost the scent, I will have to break the middle boy--or rely on Monty, the sleeper. "How could she lose it? Was it too old?"

"Nah. She can track a twelve-day-old scent when we get a strong sample. Many people handled the oilcan. The scent was not pure. Fabric he's worn close to his body works best. Next time give her a better starter scent and she'll find your man."

CHAPTER 15

IAN IGNORED the branches that switched his face and arms. He ran and ran and ran until he stumbled and fell to his hands and knees. He sucked great gulps of air. *Oh, dear God, dear God, dear God. What do I do?* Exhales turned into tiny clouds. Painful shudders racked him. He rose to his knees, rocked back and forth, and pounded his fists into his thighs. The heel of his right hand banged on hard plastic—The Handie Talkie.

Monty. His cousin's a deputy. Monty can call his cousin. He can find out where they took Travis. Ian unclipped the Handie Talkie from his belt and stopped. He smeared his hand across his face and pressed it against his mouth until his teeth threatened to cut through his lip. He'd sworn he would never endanger Monty again.... He clipped the Handie Talkie back in place and climbed to his feet.

The County Sheriff could take Travis to any of five jail-houses. *I can't search all those places.* He paced a figure eight around two trees. They could take Travis to the Second Sphere.

The knot of lava in his guts soared up through his stomach to his chest and burst out of his throat in a silent ceaseless scream. Eventually, the pain dulled enough he could think again.

First thing's first. Find Travis. He picked up the Handie

Talkie again, turned it on, and pushed the broadcast button. "Calling Blackbird. This is Thorn. Come in, Blackbird."

Static answered.

He called over and over until his voice was hoarse.

"Thorn. This is Blackbird. Are you there, Thorn? Go ahead. Over."

"They got him. I gotta find him."

"Say again. Who's got who?"

"Silver Thorn—the Sheriff took him. I don't know where he is."

"Why did the—never mind. Where are you? Over."

Ian glanced around. "I don't know."

"Meet me at the GTH?"

"It's not safe there."

"I'll come to you. Where?"

Ian struggled to think. He couldn't be too far from the Parkway. "Otter Lake Waterfall Overlook. Hurry."

"Calm down, Thorn. I'm close. Give me about ten minutes. I'll be there. Over and out."

"See you in ten. Out." He switched off the radio and took off.

He got there before Monty.

The overlook parking area was an unlit, vacant patch of asphalt surrounded by a split-rail fence. From it, a five-hundred-foot-long asphalt path led to the waterfall.

He paced across the dew-slicked grass from the trees to the parking area fence and back again. He glanced at his watch at least fifty times.

The growl of a car engine approached.

He hid in the trees.

A Rambler-shaped sedan pulled into the parking area. The engine died and someone climbed out of the car but left the headlights on. "Thorn? Are you out there?"

It is Monty. Ian released his pent-up breath and called, "Douse your lights."

A moment later the lights went out.

Ian rushed out of the trees and words tumbled out of him before he reached Monty's side. "You have to call your cousin, find out where they took him."

"Slow down." Monty grabbed him by the arms. "Who took who?"

"Travis. They grabbed Travis. Chased me. I couldn't follow him. I don't know where he is."

"Who grabbed Travis? Where?" Monty spoke loud and slow, enunciated each syllable.

Ian released a shuddering breath. "A couple of Bedford County Sheriff's deputies. We robbed Dixie's Gas and Food Mart. We got away but—" He needed to hit something. He twisted free from Monty, turned and brought his fists down on the hood of the car. The metal rang. "Stupid Twinkies. I dropped them. Travis went back—They grabbed him." He stuffed his fist in his mouth, paced away, then turned to Monty. "I can't let them Take him. Not Travis, too. I gotta find him. Call your cousin. Help me find him."

"Okay—okay," Monty said. "Calm down. I'll call my cousin. We'll find out where Travis is." He circled the front of the car, opened the passenger door. "Get in."

Ian stowed his bulging rucksack in the back, then slumped low in the front passenger seat like a shamed dog.

Monty slammed the door, dashed around the car, jumped into the driver's seat.

The engine grumbled and snarled. Tires screamed against the asphalt.

They fishtailed onto the highway.

"Where are we going?"

"I passed a Sinclair station with a phone booth. I'll call Jerry from there."

Ian nodded, closed his eyes. Mental snapshots haunted his memory. There was the day he'd taught Travis how to bait his own hook and the giant grin on his face when he caught his first I-did-it-myself fish. The worshipful gaze Travis gave him after he'd used firecrackers to blow up their green plastic soldiers followed. And the wild-eyed terror on his face when the deputy dragged him into the car—the pain in Ian's chest deepened. He opened his eyes and focused his gaze outside.

The round, white Sinclair sign with its green dinosaur appeared in the visible wedge of the windshield.

"Stay low." Monty pulled into the gas station and parked. "I'll get Jerry to find Travis." He reached for the door handle, hesitated, then got out.

Hoping he'd be able to hear Monty, Ian cranked the window down an inch.

A creak and screech of metal doors and the rumble of plastic had to belong to the phone booth. Ian rose up and peered over the lower edge of the passenger window.

Monty stood in an aluminum-framed telephone booth, his voice an unintelligible murmur. His brows pulled in and he frowned, shook his head. His murmur grew louder but no less unintelligible. Then, his face smoothed and his voice mellowed. He hung up the phone and opened the creaky door.

Ian dropped back down and cranked the window closed.

Monty climbed into the car. "Stay down."

He put the car in reverse, then pulled onto the Parkway again.

Inside Ian screamed for Monty to tell him what he'd learned, but he knew Monty would tell him when it was safe to talk. The tires whirred against the pavement for interminable seconds.

"Jerry says the patrol car happened to pass the store. Movement and a light caught their eye. They arrested an underage kid but surrendered him to the Second Sphere."

Ian moaned and thumped his forehead against the dashboard.

"It's okay. Jerry told me where the agents took Travis."

He stopped banging his head.

"They're in that old abandoned church on Elon Road."

He released his breath. "I can't defeat a bunch of Second Sphere agents."

"Not a bunch—four. And it's we. We'll defeat them."

"I can't ask you to—"

"You didn't."

The ache in Ian's chest and throat blocked the words he wanted to say.

"It'll take us about fifteen minutes to get there."

Monty ignored speed signs and drove downhill fast, slewed around curves.

"Is your father's hunting rifle in the trunk?"

"Yeah. But one rifle, four agents. Not great odds."

After a hard left onto Elon Road, Monty slowed and turned off his headlights. He took a sharp right and they did a bone-bruising bounce down an unlit dirt road.

After Monty shut the car off, the engine coughed and pinged.

Ian met Monty at the back of the car. Something lightweight brushed his hair. He swiped at it and found nothing.

Monty popped open the trunk. A tiny light lit the green carpet interior. An olive cartridge case and a black rifle case lay in a custom rubber tray. He unzipped the rifle case and pulled out a thirty-ought-six Winchester hunting rifle.

"Honestly, I think I should go alone—you don't need to be involved."

"Four to one? Talk about bad odds—" In the glow of the trunk light, Monty gave him a not-going-to-happen face. "You need me.

I've been to this church. I know the layout." He opened the cartridge case, then opened the breach of the rifle and fed a round into the rifle's chamber.

Taken aback, Ian cocked his head. "You've been to this church?"

"It's abandoned. Dad and I use it for a backdrop during target practices." He clicked seven more rounds into the chamber.

In Ian's opinion that disrespected the former church as much as the Fellowship that encouraged vandalism of old churches. He shook off his distress. "Do you have a plan?"

"I'll use the rifle to engage and distract while you rescue Travis."

"How do I find him? He could be anywhere inside."

"All but three rooms are heavily damaged. Only one of those rooms has no windows." Monty grabbed a handful of cartridges and put them in his jacket pocket. He forced a small cardboard box of cartridges into his other pocket. "It's a storage room on the north side of the pulpit. I'll create a diversion out front for two minutes—longer if I can. You'll go in through a window near the pulpit and grab Travis. Get back here pronto."

He was so lucky to have a friend like Monty. "Man, I love you for being willing to do this, but you could get killed. It's better if I go alone." He reached for the rifle.

Monty pulled the rifle close to his chest and put his other hand on Ian's shoulder. It was too dark to read Monty's expression, but his eyes locked with Ian's. "Brothers help brothers. That's what this mission is all about."

The tiny straw that was Ian's throat narrowed. All he could do was nod.

They crept through the trees toward the church. A raindrop hit his cheek. Ian caught his curse before it left his throat.

Through the trees, Ian glimpsed the marquee that had once

touted the topic of Sunday's sermon. His skin crawled with the heebie-jeebies. Every ounce of his being screamed wrong way.

"Wait," he whispered. "Change of plan. We'll go south." He turned that direction, his heebie-jeebies grew less frantic.

"But..." Monty hadn't followed him.

Ian waved him forward. Monty hesitated for a moment longer then, trotted to catch up.

When a glimpse through the trees confirmed they were parallel to the church's front doors, he caught Monty's eye and pointed toward the front.

Monty gave a thumbs-up and crept closer to the church.

Ian worked his way to the back of the building, opposite the last window.

The stained-glass windows cast multi-colored light across the littered churchyard. Behind the glass, a distant man-shaped shadow paced back and forth, back and forth.

Ian dashed from the tree line to a pile of debris where he crouched. He swallowed but it didn't moisten his throat. His legs quivered, he put a hand down to steady himself. Bricks, whole and partial, shifted. Outwardly he froze, inside his heart quivered in ribs suddenly too small. His fingers closed around a brick missing one corner. Seconds passed and no call of discovery came. He hefted the brick. It might come in handy.

The glass in the last window had been broken but much of it still hung in the frame. He took off his coat and wrapped it over his head, shoulders and arms.

The bang of the first shots startled him.

An explosion of gunshots followed. The man who'd been pacing the sanctuary moved to the front. Monty's distraction worked!

Ian leaped through the window. Glass shattered and crashed to the floor.

He ran across the pulpit to the north side. Sure enough, there was a door blocked by a heavy, three-legged table lying on its side.

"Halt!" a man called from behind him.

Ian whirled and threw the brick—hard.

The brick hit the man's face. He dropped his pistol and fell face first to the floor.

Ian spun around and called, "Travis? Are you in there?"

"Ian? Yes! In here." He knocked frantically on the wooden door.

"I'll get you out of there." Ian pushed the heavy table toward the front of the raised pulpit.

The door opened and Travis stepped out. "Man, am I glad to —Watch out!"

Ian grabbed Travis and dove behind the table.

Bullets thudded against the wood.

Pinned underneath him, Travis twitched with every thud.

Ian scanned the floor desperately hoping for bricks. No bricks--books, hymnals. He grabbed the nearest one. A bullet hit the spot where the hymnal had been.

Ian whispered, "Be ready to run, jump out that window, and head for the trees."

Travis glanced at the window, nodded.

An abrupt silence made Ian's ears ring. *Crap. Monty must be out of bullets.*

The man in the sanctuary with them took a heavy footstep closer to the altar.

A barrage of bullets rang and pinged against the brick outside.

"Now!" Ian threw the hymnal at the agent and followed Travis out the window.

Ian tucked and slid and hit the ground wrong. Flat on his back with the wind knocked out of him, he rocked like an upside-down turtle.

"Ian?" Travis called from close by.

The Second Sphere agent appeared at the window. He aimed.

Ian sucked in a breath and hoped being shot wouldn't hurt too much.

Bang-bang!

The agent screamed, grabbed his face, and vanished from the window.

Ian took one small breath, then another. It didn't hurt. He stared at his chest—no blood. "Travis?"

Travis stood motionless, wide-eyed, mouth open.

"Travis, are you okay?" Ian scrambled to his feet.

"Run!" Monty called.

Ian ran forward, grabbed Travis by the arm, and pulled. They ran together into the fog.

Monty got to the car first. The trunk stood open. "Take this," Monty said, holding out the rifle and the cartridge box.

"That's your father's—" Ian protested.

Monty shoved the rifle and bag into Ian's chest. "No time. You need this. Get in the car."

Ian gulped back a wave of emotions that were too big and took the rifle and box.

"Let's get out of here," Travis cried and climbed into the back seat.

Ian and Monty scrambled into the car. The engine roared and the car shot forward.

They rode in a thick, palpable silence of things unsaid all the way to the Quarry Road intersection.

Monty pulled over and turned to Ian.

"You saved my life," Ian said. "And Travis..." Inadequate, his words clogged his throat. "They'll hunt you down."

Monty gave him a sad smile. "No. They are hunting *you*. Get out of Virginia. After tonight—"

After tonight— Ian bit his lower lip. "We'll never see each other again." The words he couldn't say thickened, became a boulder in his gut. Ian stuck out his hand.

"Come on, Ian." Travis waited at the edge of the forest.

Monty took his hand. "Get out of the state. Now."

"I'll never forget what you did."

Monty gave him a quick salute and put the car in gear.

Ian slung on his rucksack, then jogged to the edge of the trees where Travis waited. *You said your piece. Keep going.* He nodded at Travis and entered the forest without looking back.

CHAPTER 16

THE VEINS IN WILLIAMS' temples thundered. He didn't bother keeping his voice down. "You could have killed my agent!" His words didn't echo in the empty sanctuary anymore. Too many broken windows.

Monty wore a chagrined expression. "I shot the brick. He leaned out of the window and accidentally got peppered with shards of the brick."

"And you *accidentally* found a gun?" He glowered at Monty.

"My Dad keeps his hunting rifle in the trunk. Ian knew that, sir. I kept it from him. But I have my cover, my family's cover, to protect— I had to act like I was helping."

"You *did* help him." Williams paced three strides away, side-stepped a lone hymnal on the floor. Glass crunched underfoot. "How did he know to go to the sanctuary storeroom?"

"An educated guess and a last-minute change of plans. I did exactly what I was supposed to. I never shot at a window or a person. I only shot the building."

Williams couldn't believe he'd allowed himself to trust a double-dealing sleeper. He spun and faced the young man. "Tell me one of the boys left a piece of clothing in your vehicle."

"No, sir. Why would they do that? Why didn't you get Travis's jacket?"

I had the boy, that's why. You cost me the middle boy. Maybe my life.

"They were both in my father's car—sitting on cloth seats. Will that work?"

It might. "Adler!"

Adler poked his head between the sanctuary doors. "I've already called."

"Keys."

Monty hesitated, then dropped his car keys into Williams's hand.

Williams grabbed his topcoat. Monty followed him. "Where do you think you're going?"

"It's my father's car, sir."

"You'll ride with Adler."

————

Williams pulled over at the Quarry Road intersection. Fischer stood beside his old black pickup waiting with his bloodhound, Xena. She lay on the ground as if she were too tired to lift her head. Williams swallowed. He was risking his life on the nose of an ugly, long-eared dog.

He parked. Fischer opened the car's front passenger door and a rush of cold wind blew in.

"Xena, smell," he said. The dog sniffed all over the passenger seat.

Williams got out of the car.

Adler parked behind him. He and Monty came to stand beside Williams. Adler handed him a flashlight. Monty's face paled at the sight of the dog climbing all over the car.

"Wait in Adler's car."

Monty flicked an indecipherable look at Williams, then followed orders.

Once Monty was out of earshot, Williams confirmed that Adler had the keys to that vehicle. He didn't want Monty interfering again. Now, if the rain would hold off... Gray clouds covered the sky from horizon to horizon.

Finally, Fischer said, "Seek, Xena. Seek."

The dog leaped out of the car, put her head down, and crossed the ground in an apparently random fashion.

For the next hour, Williams barely kept up while the dog frantically climbed through bush after bush, following the scent.

Williams's topcoat snagged on something. He tugged on it. *Riiip!* He glowered at the piece of gray silk hanging from a prickly branch, and then straightened and studied the surrounding area. The oldest Hobart hadn't been through here. If he had there would be a piece of his clothing here, too.

The dog woofed and took off again. Williams hesitated for a half-a-second, reminded himself that he'd seen Fischer's dogs work before, and ran after the mutt.

The dog followed a fast running creek for a long while, then she went into a search pattern again.

Adler consulted the map he carried. "Thompson Creek."

The dog darted up and down the firm ground leading up to the water's edge. There were no footprints.

Even the dog is stumped. "Is this the end of the trail, Fischer?"

Fischer shook his head. "No. She follows the scent in the air —she'll find where he crossed, then we cross, too." Clouds scudded overhead again.

Xena ran up and down the creek then plunged in and across to the other side. Fischer waded across. Adler hesitated and glanced a question at Williams.

Williams gestured toward the creek. "We either follow the dog or give up."

"Yes, sir." Adler stepped into the creek and gasped. "It's cold, sir."

Forewarned, Williams spared his dignity and held in his gasp. The rushing artic water swirled around his knees

He hadn't even dried from the creek when something stung his face. Sleet. Gentle at first, it pelted him faster and harder.

Up ahead, Fischer and the dog took shelter under a tall pine tree. Williams joined them. Adler, too. They stood close to the trunk, sheltered from the tiny pellets of ice that beat the trees and bounce across the ground.

"We are done," Fischer shouted over the clatter of ice. "The weather is too dangerous for Xena and for us."

Williams shook his head. "No. We have to be close—we have to press on."

"On ice, on a mountain, in the dark, Willie?" Fischer's face puckered in a deep frown. "I will run the dog in the rain or snow, but I will not risk her, or myself, on ice."

"Will the dog be able to follow the scent when this melts off?"

"Not the old trail." He stroked her head. "But preserve the vehicle. She will find the new trail." Fischer's wide smile projected his confidence.

"Good. We'll bring the men back in the morning. In the daylight after this melts, we will be able to search more thoroughly." As *limited as my resources are, I have three men, and Fischer and his dog, and a sleeper. Not enough.* But the Hobarts have less. They are on their own.

CHAPTER 17

THE SLEET FORCED Ian and Travis to take shelter in a thick grove of pines. At first, he was thankful, certain the icy conditions would send their pursuers home. But the storm didn't let up for hours.

Between the Sterno and the stolen winter coats, they stayed relatively warm and dry. But they used all the Sterno. Unable to sleep, when the storm stopped they headed for the cave.

Ian slipped and windmilled his arms ineffectively against the weight of the rucksack pulling him backward. He caught a branch and his balance. The branch creaked and ice pelted him. Under the trees was safer than out in the open where ice covered every step, but surprise slick spots lurked in the shadows.

"Oof!"

Ian turned cautiously. "Are you okay?"

"Nothing broken." Travis crawled to the nearest trunk, used it to regain his footing.

Ian slowed their pace. They couldn't afford a broken bone or concussion from a fall.

A peek through a gap in the trees revealed the clouds on the horizon backlit with weak sunlight. Dawn. He was late. He prayed Leslie wouldn't leave until the last minute.

They followed the creek that gurgled and rushed down the middle between the ice covering the slower water next to each bank. The fissure came into view, a dark slash in the rocky wall. He reminded himself that its depth kept the light hidden. Leslie could still be there.

She met them inside, at the opening of the fissure. "Oh, thank God. Two minutes later and we would have been gone. The storm had me worried." Her voice showed the strain and tears glistened in her eyes, but she didn't cry. "Come warm up by the fire. Where were you?"

"I got caught and Ian saved me!"

"Monty helped," Ian said. "Without him, we might both be dead."

"What?" Leslie shot a horrified look from Travis to Ian.

Ian's legs trembled. He crossed over to the fire pit, slid the heavy, wet rucksack off his back, and sank to his knees. Leslie hurried to the stack of packed belongings by the cave entrance, unrolled a quilt and a sleeping bag, and offered one to Ian and the other to Travis.

Ian wrapped the sleeping bag around his shoulders and promised himself he wouldn't sleep. The minute the sun melted the ice they had to get out of here.

"We watched the store for hours..." Travis relayed the night's events.

Leslie dug an extra log out of a dark corner and put it on the fire.

"—I ran back for the Twinkies. I had them, too. But I dropped them when the deputy grabbed me." He curled forward and gave Ian an apologetic glance.

Ian pulled Travis to him and knuckle-rubbed his head. "I should have stopped you."

"He locked me in the car until they stopped searching for you."

"Did he hurt you?" Leslie asked.

Travis's face clouded and he rubbed his left shoulder. "Not much."

Leslie pulled his t-shirt neck to inspect his shoulder. Faint red-purple fingerprints showed where the man had grabbed him.

"I was in jail for a while, then another guy came. He took me to that old church and shut me in that room." His voice dropped. "He argued with another man, his boss, I think. Anyway, this guy was angry. Every other word he shouted Ian's name."

Leslie turned to Ian. "Why would he do that?"

Ian tried to look clueless. *My article must have been closer to the truth than I knew.*

"Anyway, I sat down to wait." He beamed at Ian. "I knew you'd find me. And you did."

"Monty found you," Ian said.

"Thank God!" Leslie gave Travis a long hug.

"We brought a ton of food back. Can we eat now? I'm hungry," Travis said.

Leslie laughed. "I'll fix you something." She rummaged in the rucksack a moment then clapped her hands. "Look at all this food! I'll fix you whatever you want."

The aromas of fire-roasted Spam and pork and beans for breakfast finally woke Kenny.

Ian scarfed down the Spam and beans like he hadn't seen food in a month.

He watched Leslie finish eating. Face drawn, dark circles under her eyes, and a smudge of soot across her forehead, she appeared far older than sixteen.

His chest constricted and hardened. Gentle, never-hurt-a-soul, neatnik Leslie shouldn't have to live like this. He clenched his fists until his fingernails dug into his palms.

She tore her gaze from watching Travis and Kenny rough-housing in their sleeping area, turned to him, and whispered,

"They were going to use Travis for bait to get the rest of us, weren't they?"

"Yeah." Leslie was smart and practical. He needed to remember that.

"I don't understand," Leslie said. "Why are we here? Not here, in the cave, I mean here—alive. Why didn't they Take us, too?"

"Why did they Take Ma, Pop, and Junior?"

A shadow passed over Leslie's face. She hugged herself and curled forward. "Pop hated the Fellowship. He refused to make the store exclusive for Fellowship members."

"Yeah, but he wasn't skulking around and fighting like the rebels. And Ma sure as heck didn't hurt anyone. All Junior wanted was to heal people's pets." *Maybe I'll join the rebels.*

She poked at the fire with a long, gnarly stick. Sparks flared. Embers glowed hotter. "Travis said they were mad at you—" She watched him out of the corners of her eyes.

"I don't get that either." Painting the water tower and an article Mr. Collins said wasn't good couldn't be the reasons for all the bad stuff that happened.

"I keep going over it in my head," Leslie said. "Pop worked long hours every day, except Sunday. And Sundays we all went to the mountains, or to a neighborhood barbecue, or sat in our backyard—" Her voice caught. She turned her head away and sniffed.

He cracked the knuckles of his right hand. The only person he knew that might know how to find the rebels was Collins. He had written an article about them last year. But Ian still didn't know whether Collins was friend or foe.

"It's obvious the Second Sphere wants you—us—bad." Leslie's voice had a coarseness to it. "They'll keep searching. When the ice melts, we should leave." She glanced around the cave as if she would miss it.

"Yeah." They should leave now, get ahead of the Second Sphere, but he was stupid tired, he would make a mistake.

"So, we're going to Buena Vista?"

"No." Monty was right. They needed to leave the state. "White Sulfur Springs."

Leslie gasped. "That's a hundred miles away."

Walking that far, the four of them would be conspicuous... and easy to catch. "In three or four days, we'll pass near Glasgow." Though a small town, he'd find a Glasgow grocery and rob it. Maybe he'd find a dime. Maybe he'd find the rebels.

After lunch, Ian wriggled out of the fissure and stopped, stunned by the unseasonably cold blast of air and the sparkling gray and white world before him. Every tree and bush and blade of grass bent under the weight of ice. Broken limbs littered the ground. *This is November, not January.* It wasn't January cold, but he was grateful for his stolen jacket. He retreated inside.

"We're not going anywhere today." He gave Leslie a rueful smile. "Lots of ice, still. Too little sun and it's really cold."

Ian shrugged off his rucksack. "Don't unpack anything except what we need for today."

Leslie laughed. "We don't have anything but what we need."

Ian inspected the rifle Monty had given him. Two rounds in the chamber and twenty-eight rounds in the box. He glanced at Kenny and Travis playing tic-tac-toe in the dirt. He'd save the ammo for defense.

————

By the end of the day, a rock of what-will-we-do-if-this-continues settled into Ian's gut. He took a log from their dwindling supply and put it on the coals. It hissed and popped.

A few minutes later, the smell of roasting hot dogs filled the cave. Ian repositioned the stick so his hot dog browned on the other side and swore he'd never take hot food for granted again.

"Can I have another—er, may I?" Kenny pointed his stick at Leslie.

Leslie raised an eyebrow at Ian.

He nodded. He could steal more in Glasgow. His throat tightened and his pulse quickened. *We won't get caught. The Second Sphere won't expect to find us in Glasgow.*

CHAPTER 18

IAN TOOK the former tuna can with its meager portion of soup from Leslie and went out to the creek bank. After two weeks in the cave, he relished the cool, fresh air on his face for the second day in a row. The sun's bright rays warmed his skin.

Yesterday's rapid thaw had filled the air with loud creaks and cracks and crashes. Today the creek bubbled and gurgled, the birds chirruped, and squirrels scolded.

He scanned the terrain. Most of the ice had melted everywhere except in the deepest shadows. Leslie had been right. Today was warmer. Safer.

"When I grow up, I'm going to make a zillion dollars," Kenny said.

Travis snickered.

"I'll have scads of bacon and eggs and biscuits and ice cream. And we can eat it whenever we're hungry—even you, Travis." Kenny slurped soup from his tuna can bowl.

After two days of freezing rain and snow, he had rationed their food. The others had been angry at first. Good thing he did. None of them had imagined that the freeze would last two weeks.

"Quit talking about food." Daggers of resentment filled Travis's glare directed at Ian.

"That would be nice, Kenny." Hunger gnawed at Ian, too. And the fifty-mile hike to West Virginia wouldn't help.

The freeze had undoubtedly killed the edibles he'd counted on to feed them. And the trip held enough hazards they may not have a future.

Fortunately, the cold had slowed the fish in the creek. Or Travis's spearfishing had improved. He'd managed to spear a couple of mountain trout two days in a row.

The smell of fish roasting over the fire had driven everyone crazy with hunger. They resented the scant portions he allotted each of them for their dinners, unaware that he hungered as much as they. Leslie packed the rest in the last of the aluminum foil. Packed it for their hike to Glasgow.

Leslie joined them on the creek bank. She set the A&P Grocers tote on dry ground. "Before you ask, the fire is out." She avoided eye contact with him, crossed her arms, and frowned at the water.

Finished with his soup, Ian washed his can in the creek, shook out most of the icy water, then packed it in the A&P bag.

They had pounded the cans' sharp edges and turned tuna cans into bowls and the taller ones into drinking cups and cooking vessels. They needed forks and spoons.

One at a time, his siblings rinsed their tuna can bowls in the creek and then packed them.

Kenny picked up the roll of quilts, wriggled into the rope harness Ian had created for him. He beamed, chin in the air. "I'm ready."

Travis and Ian picked up their respective rucksacks and Leslie the cloth A&P bag that rattled with the food and the remainder of their possessions: the can opener, matches, batteries, and their tin can dishes.

A deep breath and its slow release didn't ease the tension in Ian's muscles. He forced a smile. "It's time." He took off, tried not to, but had to glance behind him. The others followed. Somehow, that didn't ease his tension.

———

Ian led them around downed trees, broken limbs, and mud and ice. He huddled in his stolen coat keenly aware that none of their clothing would save them from the extremes of winter in the mountains. They needed hats and scarves and sweaters.... Crossing the valley would be ten degrees warmer than here in the mountains. But after those nine or ten miles, there were taller, more rugged mountains to cross before they reached West Virginia. His stomach tightened. He'd have to rob a food mart *and* a clothing store in Glasgow to get everything they needed.

They reached a flat expanse of patchy grass and volunteer saplings. The Blue Ridge Parkway had been one of President Garner's New Deal creations. Only the southern half of the road had been completed when the New Deal fell through. This flat expanse was what remained after the trees had been cut and the road graded.

On the other side of the parkway, the grade grew steeper. A trail through the brush and trees and fallen leaves led up at an angle fit for a mountain goat.

"Ian, we need to rest." Leslie stood beside Kenny who sat Indian-style on a rocky protrusion, his ruddy face dripped sweat and his shoulders heaved with each breath.

Already? Eyes raised to the sky, he counted to five and tried not to sound irritated. "We can't stop yet. If we stop every two hours, we'll—"

After a glare, Leslie smoothed her expression. "Shorter legs work harder than yours, take two or three times more steps than you."

True enough. Okay. Frequent—short—breaks. "We'll take a five-minute water break."

Sunshine dappled the muddy ground between gnarled shadows of bare branches and large dark cones of the pines. Travis sank on the rock next to Kenny. Nearby, Leslie sat on another partially exposed boulder.

Ian opened the canteen he carried and handed it to Kenny. "Just one or two small swallows for now."

Kenny obeyed and handed the canteen to Travis who drank and handed it to Leslie.

Aroo Arrooo.

Gooseflesh raised on Ian's arms. He put a finger to his lips.

Travis and Leslie gave sidelong glances at the trees that surrounded them. Kenny clapped his hands over his mouth.

It could be a dog hunting coons. Ian hoped—prayed—pleaded —let it be a coon dog.

The next baying came from further away. He huffed out a breath. "We're okay," he whispered without meaning to. He raised his voice to a normal level. "We should leave now."

Kenny didn't argue.

Travis swallowed hard and stood and slipped his rucksack back on.

The boys fell in line behind him and Leslie brought up the rear.

The climb grew steeper. He tossed glances over his shoulder from time to time. Kenny struggled. Sometimes he had to put his hands down on the ground to climb.

Leslie caught up with him, touched his arm. "Are we off course?" She didn't whisper but kept her voice low and intimate.

"No—Going around the mountain. It'll add a couple of miles, but I think we should stay as far from the road as possible."

Her inhale was audible. "You think the dog hunts for us, don't you?"

If dogs are hunting us, we can't get far enough away fast enough. "I think we have to take extra precautions."

She bit her lower lip but said nothing else and fell back in line behind him.

He concentrated on putting one foot in front of the other.

CHAPTER 19

CAN'T STOP. The grit in Ian's eyes burned and itched. He refused to let his heavy eyelids close. They'd heard the dog again this morning. They breakfasted on beef jerky while they climbed. Ian set a fast pace but it had taken better than half the day to climb the mountain.

He glanced over his shoulder. Grim and silent, Leslie trailed him. Kenny's soft mutter came from behind her, "Stupid rocks." Travis brought up the rear.

Three days after they'd first heard the hound, they'd reached Glasgow and made camp a mile west of town. Ian and Travis snuck back into town and burglarized a small convenience store. They didn't get much and didn't hang around to try another.

They crossed the valley six weeks and three days after his parents and Junior were Taken. It was mid-December and they needed warmer clothes to climb the mountains. Their camp at the base of the mountains became a cozy HQ. Every three days a pair of the oldest siblings would walk to a small town or a farm and steal something. A pair of boots, a pair of jeans for Leslie, gloves, a hat or two, and canned meats or jerky. They needed plenty.

Yesterday, they'd heard the hound for the first time in a

couple of weeks. They packed hastily and charged up the mountain. When it grew too dark, they sheltered under a large pine tree, but none of them had slept well.

Forty-five days and their hunters had not forgotten. Ian hadn't either. He would never forget. Never stop counting the days. Never forgive.

He stumbled over a dead-fall branch and staggered for a couple of larger-than-he'd-planned downhill steps before he recovered. *Focus.* Saplings, bushes, and trees punctuated the steep and rocky terrain. Mud sucked at his shoes, tried to pull them off. *Put one foot in front of the other.* A prickle spidered down his back. The squirrels and birds had grown quiet. His muscles tensed and his heart sped up. No baying or other sounds of pursuit. He hoped the animals had quieted because of the weather and not because of a stealthy dog.

"Oh!" Kenny and then Leslie cried out.

"Watch out!"

"Quiet," Ian scolded. He half-turned toward them—something knocked his feet out from under him. He fell over Leslie and Kenny and slid and kept sliding.

Scrambling for purchase, he caught Kenny's coat and wouldn't let go. He grabbed a sapling. His shoulder screamed against the jerk that tried to tear it apart. But their downhill slide stopped.

He sat up and rubbed his aching shoulder then flexed his arms and legs. *Nothing broken.* But his right elbow and hip were tender.

Kenny sat up and rubbed the back of his head. "Ow."

"Where else does it hurt?" Ian ran a hand over Kenny's head. His skull was firm, no squishy spots or hard lumps. "Travis? Leslie?" he whispered.

"I'm okay," Travis's breathy whisper had an edge to it. He sidestepped down the slope toward them, stopped next to Ian and

Kenny and glanced around. "Leslie?" He whirled around. "Leslie?" His voice high and tight and loud.

"Whisper," Ian said, but he couldn't see her either.

His pulse doubled. "Leslie?"

No answer.

"Where are you?" He dared a stage whisper.

Still no answer. His insides tensed and trembled. He scrambled to his feet.

Slide marks led downhill, through mud and piles of dead leaves and yellowing creepers. He hurried down the trail, whispering Leslie's name every couple of feet.

A partly uprooted bush had broken branches stripped of leaves. His insides knotted tighter. *She grabbed it but couldn't hang on.*

Forty feet downhill, a cluster of uneven, barren rocks broke through the earth. The trail of mud passed over them and changed color. A rough-edged rock smeared with reddish mud stopped him. His chest and all those knots clenched tighter. *That's blood.* He ran faster.

Crumpled against a large tree trunk, Leslie lay still—scary still.

He knelt beside her. "Leslie?" the word squeezed out of his throat.

A wave of dizziness blurred his vision. He couldn't tell if she was breathing.

Her hair covered her face. He brushed it back.

Pale to the point of being gray, she squeezed her eyelids shut and panted.

Oh, thank God. She's breathing. "Leslie?"

Her lips moved soundlessly.

He lowered his head, put his ear close to her mouth.

"Broken." The weakness of her voice cranked his pulse up another notch.

Please God, not her back. "What's broken?"

"Leg."

Her knees were bent and her legs looked normal but—blood pooled beneath her. His chest spasmed—*Be calm. Remember Boy Scouts, first aid.* "Can you roll onto your back?"

"Hurts."

He forced a loud whisper, "Travis—"

"We're here," Travis and Kenny stood a yard away. Kenny gaped at Leslie and hugged the mud-crusted A&P sack.

Travis came a few steps closer. "Should I find some sticks for a splint?"

Ian didn't take his eyes off Leslie. "Not yet. We need to see it first. Which leg, Leslie?"

"Left."

"I'll take care of her left leg. You help her roll over to her back."

Travis knelt and pulled on her shoulder.

Leslie cried out.

Travis jerked his hand back. "Sorry. Sorry. Sorry." He clutched his arms to his chest.

"We might hurt her some," Ian said. "But we have to stop the bleeding. If we can't turn her, we can't help her."

"I can't. I can't."

"You can. Just like when you got your first aid badge in Scouts."

His shoulders rose toward his ears and he gave a slow side-to-side headshake.

Ian locked his eyes on Travis. "She can't do it for herself. *We* have to help her."

He swallowed hard and his shoulders relaxed a tiny bit. "Okay."

"Remember, sit near her head—that's it. Hands under her shoulders. On the count of three. One-two-three."

Ian held her hip and leg bent at the same angle in relation to her body during the roll to her back.

Leslie's shrill gasp tightened his throat as if it were a noose.

He tried to say good job to Travis but his voice didn't work.

Twigs and dirt and leaves matted the left leg of her blood-soaked and torn jeans. He ignored the metallic smell and rubbed his damp palms on his thighs.

Leslie squeezed her eyelids tight in an I'm-not-going-to-cry-out-again grimace.

"Pressure to the wound." Travis's face was almost as gray as Leslie's.

Kenny's overly bright eyes darted from Ian to Travis to Leslie and back again. His chin trembled.

Ian smoothed his own worry from his face. *Can't let them panic. They need something to do.* "Travis, get the blanket—the thin one. Tear it into strips for bandages."

Travis continued to gawk at Leslie's leg.

Please. Don't make me yell at you. "Travis. Look at me—Look. At. Me."

Slowly, Travis raised his gaze.

Ian locked eyes with him. "Leslie needs bandages. Do you understand?"

Travis blinked, then nodded over and over and over like a nodder doll.

"Get the blanket out of your rucksack," Ian spoke as slow and clear as he could. "I need you and Kenny to tear it into strips about four inches wide."

"Okay." Travis took off his rucksack and dug out the ratty blanket. "How many?"

"Two dozen." He pulled the canteen off. His hands shook. He prayed he could do this without hurting her too much. "Leslie?"

She opened her eyes.

"I'm going to have to clean the wound."

She moaned through clenched teeth and gave a short nod.

Ian poured water over the wound. The water exposed the ragged gash. It curved from the outside of her swollen thigh to the top of her knee and down to her shin. An ocean of blood pooled in and overflowed the wound in seconds. *Oh, man. That's deep.*

He forced himself to assess it. *No bones sticking out. Not pulsing blood. Not an artery.* He breathed a little easier. He took a couple of blanket strips from Travis. "I'm sorry, Les—" He squeezed the edges together.

Leslie took in a sharp breath, then clamped her lips shut. Air whistled faintly in and out through her nose.

He wrapped her leg with one strip after another, tied them tight, then pressed the heels of his hands on the bandage over her thigh.

Kenny knelt beside Leslie and gave her his bedroll for a pillow. "Does Leslie need a doctor?" His soft voice shook and he stroked her hair.

Leslie opened her eyes and squared her shoulders. "I'll be okay. You three will be my doctors." But her voice quivered and her eyes sought Ian's.

He hid the oh-crap panic that threatened to overwhelm him with a fake reassuring smile. The blue blanket strips he pressed to her leg had already grown red and warm and sticky with her blood. *She needs stitches—bad. I'd trade my sleeping bag for a first aid kit or a sewing needle right now. And soap. And antibiotics.*

His fingers tingled and his arm muscles trembled but he didn't dare stop pressing on her wound. Crazy scenarios played in his head—scenarios where he tried to carry Leslie over the mountains, where hounds tracked her blood, and—digging a grave. He shook his head and tried to focus. His gaze landed on the sack Kenny clutched to his side.

"You brought Leslie's sack. Did you find it up there?"

Kenny nodded and held it out toward him.

"Is there anything left in it?"

He nodded again.

Travis put a hand on Kenny's shoulder. "Everything spilled out but we picked it up."

"Tell me what's in there."

Travis searched through and named what was in the bag. The four tuna can bowls and the can opener were missing.

Oh, God. They could be anywhere—uphill or down. "We can't leave anything behind—someone might find them."

Travis's eyes bulged and his mouth dropped open. "I'll find them."

"Good." He didn't think asking Travis to cover up the trail of blood would be wise. He'd have to do that—in a while.

Travis started uphill, stopped, and turned a solemn look on Ian. "I'll cover the trail, too."

Ian stared at his younger brother, his smile more genuine than it had been. "Good idea."

Travis turned and climbed upward.

Ian's injured shoulder ached and his fingers had gone to sleep. He glanced at his watch. Ten minutes. If the bleeding hadn't stopped by now.... He suppressed a shudder and eased up on the pressure he exerted on Leslie's thigh.

She moaned and gasped for breath.

"Sorry. I'm going to let go, okay?"

She nodded.

He peeled his hands off the bandages, held them inches above her wound, and watched the bandage. Seconds ticked past, a minute, then two. He gave Leslie a real smile of reassurance. "I think it's stopped." He rocked back on his heels. His legs quivered, too fatigued to hold him. He sat beside her, stretched his legs out, and scratched an itchy place on his hand—dried blood flaked off his skin. He stared at his bloody hands as if they were something foreign.

"You can wash your hands." Kenny held the second canteen out. "Only use a little."

He gazed at his youngest brother amazed at how he'd changed in the past month. "Thanks, buddy." A handful of water did an adequate job. Time weighed on him. The dog could be catching up to them. He searched uphill.

Travis backed downhill toward them. He dragged a pine bough twice his height, sweeping the mud to obscure the evidence of Leslie's slide. Occasionally, he bent and fluffed or righted a bush. He worked his way down to them. "Some of the bushes wouldn't stand up again."

"It's not obvious that someone fell down to here. That's all that matters."

He rattled the A&P bag. "I found everything."

"That's great."

"Help me stand up."

Ian whirled to face Leslie. "Really?" The grayish color to her lips and skin had been replaced with a pale pink. Maybe she'd be okay.

"Sure." He put his arm under hers.

Her shoulders quaked and twitched.

"Take it easy." He took most of her weight.

Her face blanched. Sweat beaded on her forehead and upper lip.

Ian's stomach dropped. "You don't look so good. Maybe you should lie back down."

"No, I can do this." She clenched her teeth and braced herself. After a few moments, her face relaxed. "See? The bandage helps a lot."

Ian gently touched the strips of blanket at her thigh. Dry. No more bleeding.

She shook so hard Ian didn't want to let go but she shrugged him off. She wobbled and her face twisted in a deep wince. "See, I can still walk." She hopped, screamed, and folded.

Ian lunged and caught her under her arms.

Kenny screamed and jumped up and down, waving his hands in the air.

"Quiet, Kenny." Travis clapped one hand over Kenny's mouth, the other snaked around his younger brother and hugged him.

Ian eased Leslie to the ground. Passed out she didn't react. Her bandage turned purple then red with blood. He squatted beside Leslie, his hand over his mouth. *This is my fault. I pushed us too hard.*

A squirrel overhead scolded them.

Kenny rushed to her side and patted her face. "Wake up, Leslie. I didn't mean to do it." He looked up at Ian. His lower lip quivered. "I fell down. I hurt Leslie."

"You didn't hurt her," Ian said. "The tree did." He had to get help for her. Maybe he could steal a needle, some suture, and penicillin.

The towns between here and Glasgow were so small he doubted any of them had a doctor. They had to go to Glasgow or farther.

It would take at least eight days to walk to and from Glasgow if he went alone. In eight days her wound could close improperly or get infected. He'd have to take Leslie closer to a medical office or hospital where he could steal the things she needed.

"Should I make a travois?" Travis asked.

"Good idea. A dog travois. We'll do it together. Kenny, you stay with Leslie."

He chopped down three saplings, cut the rope into short lengths, and hoped they'd find another rope before they needed one.

They lashed the ends of two of the saplings together. At the halfway point, they attached a crossbar to form the shape of an A. Every six inches from there, they added crossbars to form the carry area, leaving two feet of open clearance at the bottom. They padded the carry area with the quilts. Finally, they added a short crossbar near the top of the A as a handle.

Leslie's eyelids fluttered and her face grew whiter when they lifted her onto the travois. Ian's stomach lurched. He wished he could let her rest but they had to get away from here.

They covered her with a sleeping bag and as a precaution, lashed her to the travois with the last of their rope.

Ian stepped inside the top third of the A, grabbed the handle-bar, and lifted the travois. She wasn't as heavy as he had expected and the lashings held. He nodded at Travis.

Travis led, followed by Kenny who insisted that it was now his job to carry the A&P bag. Ian pulled the travois and followed Kenny. They had a few more hours of daylight they could use to get closer to Glasgow, closer to help for Leslie, and closer to their hunters.

CHAPTER 20

IAN and his brothers walked from sun-up to sun-down. After twenty-four hours, the skin around Leslie's wound was a fiery red and warm to the touch.

Two days later, they entered the valley, and Ian handed out the last of the fish for their evening meal. The wind grew sharper and the sky darker. Thunder rumbled in the distance.

"We'll take shelter in the first barn we find," Ian said.

They forced their weary legs to march onward.

Kenny stumbled and fell to his knees.

Ian caught his breath. "Travis, stop."

Travis stopped, turned, and hurried to Kenny's side. "Are you all right?"

Kenny sat up with his legs out in front of him. "My feet are too heavy."

"Let him sit with me." Leslie's voice startled Ian. She'd slept most of the day.

Ian picked Kenny up and carried him to the travois, had him sit next to Leslie's good leg. "You get to ride for a while." He strained to pick up the travois again. The extra weight made it harder to handle.

Travis walked beside him, lending a hand when he needed

more *oompf* to pull the travois over a rock or thick clump of grass. They skirted fenced farmland and avoided the lights of houses.

Night fell quickly, aided by the growing thunderclouds. Ahead, a distant halo of lights shimmered above the trees—Glasgow. The halo became their north star.

Lightning flashed and thunder rumbled closer. Ian finally spotted the dark form of a barn in an open field a hundred yards to their north and hurried them to it.

Abandoned, the barn's red paint had faded and peeled away. Its boards were worn and ragged and its partially open doors hung unevenly on their hinges. Both Ian and Travis had to shoulder the door to force it open wide enough for the travois. Inside, strange dark shapes of long abandoned things filled the barn. It smelled of dust and mold and of the coming rain.

The broken roof riddled with holes meant that only the area under the loft would stay dry. But all manner of junk had been piled under the loft: old doors and broken, rusted equipment, old barrels, and bits and pieces of nail-studded plywood and two-by-fours.

Ian set the travois down and checked on Leslie. She roused slightly and he gave her a sip of water. By the time he straightened from that, Travis and Kenny had already pulled some junk out from under the loft. They laid a discarded door against a pile they'd created directly below the front edge of the loft.

"What are you doing?"

"We're making a fort," Kenny said brightly.

Travis and Kenny dragged a rusted oil drum to the "wall."

It would hide them and keep them warmer. "That's a great idea," Ian said. "But all good forts have a bolt hole." Some critter had already created a hole in the far corner. Ian widened it enough for the travois. Then, he covered the hole with a warped sheet of plywood which he braced with one of the rusted oil drums. "If you have to get out, pull the plywood like this and go."

Travis demonstrated he could do it and then helped Ian drag the travois to the most sheltered corner under the loft. Ian dug a small Dakota fire hole and chopped up some of the old lumber for the fire. The boys raked the thin layer of straw on the floor into a sleeping bag-shaped pile. As soon as they'd placed their sleeping bag, Kenny and Travis climbed in.

Leslie's skin was on fire. She jerked and moaned at his touch. Ian peeled back the bandage. A sour smell hit him. Thick yellow-white pus filled her wound. Acid churned in his stomach. He rewrapped her leg.

"You were going to steal some medicine for her, weren't you?"

Ian started and whirled on Travis. "You should be asleep."

"She needs a real doctor."

Ian studied his brother's profile noting how thin and hollow his face looked in the light and shadow. "We can't pay for one." He wished he could talk to Leslie—she'd have an idea.

Face drawn, Travis turned his gaze on Leslie.

Ian pulled Monty's Handie Talkie out of his rucksack. He didn't even know if Monty had avoided detection after rescuing Travis. Contacting Monty again could put him in incredible danger. But he could bring money for a doctor—and food. An hour to get here, plus the time needed to gather the money and food— Ian turned the radio on.

Static sputtered erratically. The needle on the dial bounced but didn't leave the red zone. The connection was very weak. *Batteries*—he'd stolen some. He dug in his rucksack and found the batteries, size C. Right for the flashlight, wrong for the Handie Talkie.

"Blackbird, this is Thorn. Come in Blackbird." After the third attempt, he simply said his piece and hoped Monty could hear him. "Leslie's hurt. She needs a doctor. We need help. Next contact at seven a.m." He repeated the message twice and turned the radio off to conserve what was left of the battery.

The plink-plop of rain hit the barn, fell through the holes. A thunderclap startled them all. Moments later the storm rattled the loose boards of the barn like an angry mob intent on destroying it.

CHAPTER 21

WILLIAMS STUDIED the map that hung on the back wall of the sanctuary, next to the double doors to the foyer. Kerosene lamps blazed on candle stands at each end of the map, canceled out his cast shadow, and filled the room with their pungent odor. Seven weeks ago he would not have believed he would be still searching for the Hobarts, much less searching on horseback.

The ice storm had only temporarily saved him from the Major. And it hadn't saved him from the wrath of Monty's father. Monty senior had demanded reparations for the family car he couldn't retrieve until the mountain roads had been cleared and for the frostbite he claimed that Monty had suffered. The fact that neither Williams, or Adler, or Fischer had frostbite didn't calm him. The fact that Williams would pay no reparations enraged him.

The day after the ice storm, Williams had tried to rent horses. The stable owners had refused to rent the horse until the ice had melted. By then most of the roads had reopened and the ice had effectively erased the children's scents.

Williams crossed out one of the red Magic Marker squares on the map. Drawn over the white and blue lines that represented

roads and rivers or creeks, each square, a mile on each side, represented a week of searching. Five squares wide by ten long. And
only seven squares had been crossed out. *Fischer's dog had better
find a fresh scent soon.*

Seven weeks searching for four children. Five of those weeks
had been under the calculating eye of Major Banks. Banks had
flown in two days after the big thaw after Williams, Fischer, and
Adler had spent two extraordinarily long days riding horses in
pursuit of the Hobarts.

Williams watched Banks out of the corner of his eye. A short,
bull-necked man, the Major sat in the pulpit chair behind the
repaired altar table. A stack of folders sat to his left. Periodically
he'd take a folder from that pile, open it, read it, and move it to a
smaller stack of folders on his right.

The Major had approved of Williams's decision to terminate
Yardley for sleeping on the job but insisted there still were no
replacements available. Banks rode as one of the men until Nickerson had been given an eye patch and was cleared to ride.

Three days ago, Nickerson and Fischer had discovered the
cave.

Williams tapped the pin with a red flag that marked the
cave's location on the map.

*I hadn't been convinced the Hobarts had been there until the
dog dug up the fire pit.*

He figured that the Hobarts had survived the two weeks of
bitter cold after the ice storm there. They'd abandoned it weeks
before Williams's team found it. Still, Fischer had been hopeful
the dog would find a scent in the area. That had been three
days ago.

Sixteen hours a day, Fischer and the dog led the team
through a sea of rocks and trees, creeks and hollows, bald knobs
and steep inclines. Nickerson rode with him now. Soon,
Williams would take fresh horses to them. Nickerson would

return with the first set of horses, and then it would be Adler's shift.

The sanctuary doors banged open.

Startled, Williams peered into the dark doorway.

The boarded up, broken windows kept the church warmer but also created stark contrasts of light and dark. The light of the kerosene lamps didn't reach the doorway.

"What is this? Whoever you are, show yourself," Banks demanded.

Monty strode over to Banks's desk without so much as an "if you please" and started blathering about a Handie Talkie he'd given the oldest Hobart boy.

Williams struggled to conceal his distrust of this boy-sleeper who couldn't resist a lie.

"He tried to reach me by radio. The signal was weak—too weak to hear well but I think one of them is hurt." Monty gave Banks a look like a puppy trying to please.

Williams would not yield command of the hunt. "Do you know where they are?"

"No—but the radio's range is about nine miles in a relatively flat surface situation."

"Which we don't have here." He stretched his thin patience.

"Right. The mountains interfere with that, but there's a repeater antenna on a telephone pole on Shewey Ridge. That makes the range eighteen miles. They couldn't be any farther away than Glasgow if they're headed west." His voice held a genuine eagerness.

"That is helpful information, young man," Banks said as if Monty had delivered vital information. The Major rose and crossed to the map.

Adler measured a string the length equivalent of eighteen miles, tied a pin to one end, and the red Magic Marker at the other end.

"Measure from where the signal was received," Williams reminded him, "Monty's house in Ambrose."

"Right, sir." Adler marked an eighteen-mile radius circle.

Four men and a single dog couldn't cover that in a lifetime.

The radio squawked. Williams jumped. So did Banks and Monty. Banks had procured the radio so Nickerson and Fischer could continue the hunt and communicate with what Banks referred to as "HQ," meaning him.

"Captain Williams, sir?" Nickerson's excitement broke through the static of the airwaves.

"Williams, here, over."

"Sir—Xena found it! They haven't been gone long—um, over."

His neck warmed and his heart thumped harder. "What did the dog find?"

"A campsite outside of Glasgow, sir. Where they camped for some days, maybe weeks. It's been abandoned for a week, maybe two, but Xena's wild to chase after them. Should we wait for you or give chase, sir?"

Williams leaned toward the radio, every muscle in his body ached to jump into action. "What are your coordinates?" He scribbled them on a piece of paper, handed it to Adler.

Adler traced the longitude with his right index finger, then slid his left index finger along the latitude. He stuck a white pin in the location where the two crossed.

"Thirty minutes to pick up the horses in their trailer—thirty, maybe forty-five more to drive to Glasgow. At least ninety minutes before we can arrive," Williams said.

Banks peered at the map. "Tell your man to go forward."

"Two men and four resourceful children." Williams kept his voice bland.

"They are fifty miles from the border. Do you know what will happen if they cross into West Virginia?" Lines furrowed Banks's forehead.

They would cross jurisdictional lines. Williams did his best imitation of an unperturbed man but if the Hobarts crossed the state line, his life was over.

CHAPTER 22

THE SILENCE WOKE IAN. Through the holes in the barn, dawn's light tinted the sky. *Storm's over.* He reached over and touched Leslie's forehead. Hot. *Too hot.* He sat up.

"Is Leslie going to die?"

He turned to reassure Kenny, but the false words wouldn't come. "I'm going to get a doctor for her." He wished he'd been injured. She'd know what to do. She was too sick to move and too sick to steal random antibiotics and hope they'd cure her. *I have to bring a doctor here.*

Kenny sat cross-legged, frowning at the piece of straw he twisted back and forth.

Beside him, Travis sat with his elbows propped on his knees, chin in his hands. "When Junior went to school, he worked for a doctor in Glasgow, right?"

"A veterinarian, not a medical doctor." Ian grabbed the Handie Talkie.

"But he has medicines and Junior said he was a good doctor and a good man."

Ian rocked back on his heels and gaped at his brother. *The Second Sphere would never guess we used a vet.* "Do you remember the doctor's name?"

Travis gave a huge sigh, his shoulders drooped. "I hoped you did."

"Don't worry. I'll look him up." *Phone booths stand on every other corner. And a small town like Glasgow wouldn't have two veterinarians.* The Handie Talkie's needle still danced in the red. *If someone left their change in the payphone—I can call Monty.* He turned off the radio and tucked it back into the rucksack.

I'll need to travel fast. He picked one of the canteens. Water sloshed inside. The second canteen was lighter, he slung it over his shoulder. After a moment's thought, he placed one of the blanket strips in his pocket. "Now all I need is a measly dime," he muttered.

"You can have mine." Kenny held out his hand. A dime sat in his grimy palm.

Stunned speechless for a second, Ian sputtered, "Where did you get that?"

"Ma gave it to me."

"Why?"

"To buy an ice cream."

Ian gave a quick half-laugh. "An ice cream?"

"'Cause I got all A's and B's on my report card."

"I don't know when I'll be able to buy you an ice cream."

"It's okay. It's too cold for ice cream right now anyway."

Ian took the dime.

Now to find a phone booth.

"Travis, I'm trusting you to look after Leslie and Kenny. This..." He slipped the canteen strap over Travis' head, "is full, but it's all got. It has to last all day—and maybe tomorrow."

Travis raised his chin. "Got it."

He picked up the rifle, hesitated. Travis would try, but pulling the travois was too slow to escape. If anyone found them, they'd have a better chance if they could defend themselves. He handed Travis the rifle. "Stay inside the barn. And don't use this unless—"

"I see the whites of their eyes," Travis finished solemnly.

————

Ian sauntered across the railroad tracks and into Glasgow. The quiet of the stores and the street spooked him. No phone booths were in sight. *Surely Glasgow has one.*

About one-hundred-fifty yards down the street, a huge oval Esso sign perched on rooftop scaffolding. *Gas stations always have a phone booth. He hurried forward.* The white building shimmered in the bright sunlight. Behind the large plate glass windows, a station attendant sat with his feet on the desk. His feet tapped the rhythm of faint gospel music. One gasoline and one diesel pump sat unused in the drive and both garage bay doors were open, the bays vacant. One lone vehicle sat in the parking lot. *Ian guessed it belonged to the attendant.*

At the edge of the parking lot stood a blue and white, enclosed telephone booth.

An address and one short phone call. Easy peasy. Except his hands shook like he was about to commit a crime and he wanted to run the opposite direction. He walked across the street as casually as he knew how.

He pushed the phonebooth's bi-fold doors closed. Dangling from a black wire, in a hard black binder, was the blue and yellow telephone directory for Glasgow and area. He flipped through the pages.

During Junior's internship, the large animal vet had repeatedly treated animals regardless of their owner's religious beliefs. Junior said the vet worked miracles. Ian hoped the vet was the man Junior thought he was and hoped he had a miracle for Leslie.

An ad on the outside corner of a page read: Fur and Feathers Animal Clinic. Patrick O'Brien DMV. It had a tiny map and directions.

Ian peered over the top of the long black telephone. No one was in sight. He ripped the corner free, stuck it in his back pocket.

The Bakelite receiver chilled his already cold hand. He dropped Kenny's dime in the slot. The metallic clink-clink of the coin dropping gave way to a dial tone, and he dialed Monty's number. He let the phone ring twice then hung up. If Monty was home, he'd answer the phone the next time it rang. The dime clanged into the coin return box. Ian put the coin back in the slot and dialed again.

"Hello?"

"Thank goodness you're home."

"Um. Yeah, I'm home. Um, hang on a minute." Muffled, he said, "I'll take this upstairs."

Ian waited.

"Okay, Mom, you can hang up." The line clicked. "I thought I'd never hear from you again. Are you all right? How's everyone?"

"We're okay." He had intended to tell Monty about Leslie. But somehow, he couldn't.

"You don't sound okay."

"Look, I need your help again. I know it's asking a lot, but we're starving."

"I can raid the food pantry again. I'll bring it to you."

"Can you bring it to Glasgow today?"

"Sure, man. Where?"

"Put it in one of those green trash bags. Take Blue Ridge Road west out of Glasgow. After you cross the railroad track, toss the bag into the ravine. I'll get it when the coast is clear."

"I can bring it straight to you. Where are you staying?"

Ian wanted to tell Monty but he couldn't. He chewed his lower lip.

"At least tell me you've got some shelter or something."

Ian leaned his forehead against the cold glass of the booth. "We're in an abandoned barn—it's safer you don't know where. Just dump the bag at the corner. Please. I promise I won't ask for help again."

"It'll take a little while before I can get there. Dad's at work and—"

"Oh—"

"But, I can do it before supper, say five o'clock."

"I owe you. I'll repay you—someday." His throat grew thick and stopped up.

"No need. Remember? We're family."

"I gotta go—"

Ding-ding. Ian jumped. A car stopped at one of the station's pumps. He slammed the receiver on the hook and walked away, fast.

Twenty minutes later, he stood across the street from a small brick building with a hip roof. The wooden sign over the clinic door read Fur and Feathers Animal Clinic. Patrick O'Brien DMV. Behind the clinic, at least the distance of a football field away, a white batten board farmhouse faced the opposite direction, as did Glasgow Grocery down the street.

The clinic's asphalt parking lot had one vehicle in it, a dark blue Dodge Power Wagon. *Let it be the doctor's.* Ian cracked his knuckles and shook out his hands. He strode across the street, up the steps, and pushed the door open. A buzzer rang.

Dogs barked somewhere in a back room. Cats yowled and meowed. "Be there in a minute," called a male voice.

The long front room had high windows in pale blue walls and a slight medicinal odor. Bright green plastic chairs lined three walls. No Fellowship shield on display should have eased Ian's nerves, but it didn't.

The receptionist's desk sat under an archway cut from the fourth wall. Next to it stood a door to the interior. Shelves loaded with cans and bags of cat and dog food lined the other end of the fourth wall. The barking and meowing grew less frequent. A door squeaked open and a tall, big-boned man with silver-streaked, dark hair stepped into the reception area. "How may I help you?" He wore a white doctor's coat and the authority that came with it.

"My sister got hurt—camping. She's in a bad way. She needs help." The tickle in his dry throat made his voice hoarse.

The man smiled a kind, but puzzled smile. "I may wear a white coat, but I'm a veterinarian, son. I'm afraid you need a medical doctor."

Ian didn't have to try to sound pathetic. "Please. You're the closest doctor. She can't wait. Can't you stabilize her?"

He frowned. "Where is she?"

"Not far, but we'll have to do some hiking."

The doctor pressed his lips together and studied Ian. "All right. Let me get my kit and tell my wife to reschedule my afternoon appointments." The door squeaked and he disappeared into the interior of the clinic. The dogs and cats barked and yowled.

Ian made a slow circuit of the waiting room. Dr. O'Brien couldn't recognize him. They'd never met. But he could report suspicious behavior to the Second Sphere.

One minute stretched into five. Ian's palms grew slick with sweat.

Footsteps in the back hall thumped toward him.

The interior door opened and O'Brien, laden with a black medical bag and a bulging Glasgow Grocery sack, stepped into the waiting room. "My wife insisted on sending food."

Maybe he is the good man Junior thought he was. Ian led him outside.

O'Brien surveyed the parking lot. "How did you get here?"

"I walked."

"If time is important, we'd best take my car." He crossed the parking lot and stowed the bags in the Power Wagon.

Ian hesitated, prayed he wasn't walking into a trap, then hurried after the doctor.

The engine sputtered and coughed, then caught. O'Brien backed out of his parking space and stopped at the street. "I'll follow your directions."

For the first few minutes, O'Brien tried to engage Ian in small talk, questioning where Ian was from, how long he'd been camping, and where were his parents. Ian answered with grunts or shrugs and gave him directions when needed.

The doctor stopped at a stop sign and checked for cross traffic.

An old gray Pontiac Super Chief just like the one Collins, the feature reporter from the *Chronicle*, owned approached and crossed the intersection.

Muscles tensed and ready but with nowhere to run, Ian lowered his head, afraid to look, afraid Collins would recognize him, afraid he was caught. After a few moments, he peered out the windshield. The Pontiac was gone.

A sidelong glance at O'Brien assured him that the doctor hadn't noticed. Ian's tension eased. *That was too close.*

A mile down the road, he spotted the marker stones he'd stacked on the side of the road.

After they'd passed his marker, he spoke up. "Park by that grove of trees."

The engine hissed as it cooled. The doctor got his medical kit and the grocery bag from the back, stepped to the side of the road, and looked at Ian expectantly.

Ian swiped his damp palms down his sides and unpocketed the strip of blanket. He held it stretched between his hands. "I'm sorry, but you can't know where we're staying."

O'Brien drew back. "I didn't agree to that. Are you criminals?"

"We've done nothing wrong, but if the Second Sphere questions you, you'll want to be able to say you honestly don't know where we are."

The doctor set his bags down, took the blanket strip from Ian, and tied it around his own eyes. "Do you want to double check it?"

Ian gawked at him. Then, he picked up the doctor's bags and held them out in front of the doctor. He pretended to drop them. O'Brien didn't flinch. "No need." He placed the doctor's kit in his right hand and hooked O'Brien's left arm with his. "I'll carry the other bag."

He led O'Brien through a series of turns, only a few of which were necessary. The uneven ground and the blindfold slowed them more than Ian liked. He glimpsed the dark barn, alone in the field against a backdrop of rolling mountains. Guiding the doctor to the barn, he *prayed that his siblings were still safe inside*.

The barrel of the rifle appeared over the top of a stack of two-by-fours. "Halt!"

"It's me." Ian untied the blindfold. "I've got the doctor with me."

"Thank goodness." Travis stood and lowered the rifle.

O'Brien blinked a few times and scanned his surroundings. "Where's the patient?"

"Over here." Travis stepped out of the hidden entrance.

Ian gestured for O'Brien to follow Travis, and then followed the doctor.

Kenny stood between them and Leslie, in a batter's stance

with a three-foot piece of two-by-four over his shoulder and a fierce no-one's-getting-past-me expression.

O'Brien pulled back, glanced at each of the four of them, then held his hands up in the air. "I'm here to help your sister."

A different time, Ian might have laughed.

Kenny backed up, stood next to Travis. They both kept their weapons.

O'Brien hurried around the fire to Leslie's side. He touched her shoulder.

She flinched and moaned but didn't open her eyes.

He glanced at Ian. "How long has she been like this?"

"Most of two days."

He took out a stethoscope and listened to her chest, and then focused on her leg. "Nice bandage job." He unwrapped it.

The line between his eyebrows deepened. He opened his kit. "I'm not supposed to give medications to two-legged patients." He removed two vials from his bag. "You kids, you won't tell the authorities about this, will you?" He didn't look up to see if they agreed.

He assembled a needle and syringe, then drew liquid from one of the vials into the syringe.

Ian stepped forward. "What's that?"

"Something for pain—she's going to need it." He injected it in her upper arm. She didn't even moan.

"And this—" He drew milky liquid out of the second vial. "This is an antibiotic." He injected that into her arm as well.

Ian grimaced. Leslie still didn't react.

"The pain shot needs a bit of time to work." O'Brien reached into the grocery bag. "You boys look like you could use this." He passed out wax paper wrapped ham sandwiches and a thermos of lemonade.

Ian took a bite. The taste of sweet bread and salty ham flooded his mouth and twisted his stomach. He ate the rest of the tastiest ham and cheese sandwich ever in less than two minutes.

"There's more." O'Brien shook the bag. "My wife always packs as if to feed an army."

Ian, Travis, and Kenny each ate three. Carrots sticks and apples finished their meal.

Kenny got out a fourth sandwich. "I'll share this one with Les—"

"Shh." Ian glared at his little brother. "No names."

"She'll eat later," O'Brien said.

After they'd finished eating, O'Brien cleaned Leslie's wound with an antiseptic wash from his kit, then bandaged it with a gauze wrap.

"Doesn't she need stitches?" Travis asked.

"The wound needs to drain—heal from the bottom up." He repacked his kit, picked up the grocery bag now full of waxed paper wrappings and apple cores, and stood.

Ian shook O'Brien's hand. "Thank you. I don't know what we'd have done without you."

"She's very sick." He leveled a grim look on Ian. "She should be in a hospital. But you can't take her there, can you?"

Ian met his look but didn't answer.

"Can I talk you into staying with me and my wife? We have a couple of spare rooms."

Ian wished he could say yes. He shook his head.

O'Brien gave Ian a bottle of pills. "See to it that she takes one of these with food at dinner time, bedtime tonight, and in the morning. If you miss one, give her two the next time. Come and get me at seven tomorrow morning. I'll clean her wound again."

"We'll be on our way before that," Ian said.

O'Brien shot him a stern look. "Not if you want to save her leg."

Ian's insides dropped. He cleared his throat. "I'll be there.

Seven a.m." He offered the doctor the blindfold again. "For the walk back to your car."

O'Brien nodded, tied the rag around his head, and took Ian's arm.

Ian led him through enough twists and turns to keep the barn's location a secret.

Near the grove of trees where they'd left O'Brien's car, the whoosh of a car passing made Ian jerk the doctor back deeper into the trees.

"You can't run forever," O'Brien said. "Do you have a plan?"

"I—um—"

"Don't tell me. Just promise me you'll be man enough to take care of those children."

"I'll find a safe place for them, sir. I promise."

"Good."

Ian stepped out of the trees and froze. An old gray Pontiac Super Chief sat behind the Power Wagon.

"Ian? Ian Hobart? Is that really you?" Claude Collins strode toward him.

Ian whirled and bolted into the trees.

"Ian, wait!" Collins called.

"What are you doing?" The doctor asked in a loud voice. "Don't turn away from me."

"I've got to help him. He's in big trouble."

"How do I know you aren't the trouble he's running from?"

Ian darted across the field to a clump of trees closer to the mountains. If the doctor couldn't stop Collins, he had to lead Collins as far away from the barn as possible.

He ran fast and hard until he found a thicket of Mountain Laurel. He squirmed inside of it and sat, alert for sounds of pursuit for an eternity.

Birds warbled and squirrels gibbered and the wind rustled

dry branches and leaves. The shadows grew longer and the air temperature dropped.

Climbing out of the bushes wasn't as easy as climbing into them. He swiped away the bits of twigs and leaves that clung to him and glanced at his watch. Six-thirty. *Monty should have dropped the food off by now.*

The walk back to town was a lot longer than the one this morning. About a thousand yards away from the railroad track, he spotted the green bag. *Thanks, Monty. Best friend a guy—*

A yellow coupe sat parked in a tree-lined drive. Steam rolled out of its tailpipe. A lone, shadowy figure sat in the front seat. He faced the railroad tracks.

The heebee jeebies danced across Ian's back. He turned right, took a rambling cross-country route, and reached the barn long after dark.

CHAPTER 23

IAN CROUCHED in the ditch across the street and watched the dark clinic building and the empty parking lot. Cold seeped from the ground through his skin to his bones. The sky lightened to a hazy gray. His insides twitched and knotted tighter and tighter.

At ten minutes before seven, the doctor's dark blue Power Wagon rounded the corner and pulled into the parking lot. The doctor unloaded his bag and a bulky box, then unlocked the clinic. A moment later the interior lights made the windows glow.

Ian crossed the street at seven o'clock sharp. The clinic door squeaked and animals yipped and yapped and howled and yowled.

O'Brien sat in one of the plastic waiting room chairs. He looked up from a magazine. "I was afraid you weren't coming."

Ian stayed in the open door and scanned the room. The doctor was alone. "Where'd that reporter come from? Do you know him? What did he want?"

"I never met him before. I asked him what he wanted. He said he was your friend."

"He was. But not anymore."

"He wanted to warn you about something. I didn't get any

details. I argued with him long enough to give you a good head start."

"Thanks."

"Anyway, your sister's health is what's important this morning." O'Brien stood and walked to the door. "How'd she do through the night?"

"She's still feverish. But, she slept much better." Ian followed the doctor out the door.

"The fever should pass soon." The doctor crossed the parking lot to the Power Wagon.

Ian put his hand on the door handle and hesitated. The back seat of the vehicle was piled high with lumpy blankets and Glasgow Grocery bags. "What's all that?"

"My wife wouldn't hear of my leaving you kids without some supplies."

Tension filled Ian. "You told her about us?"

"She's the soul of discretion. Besides, I only told her what she had to know."

Ian climbed into the car and tried to relax.

While he drove, O'Brien alternately hummed and sang, "On the Sunny Side of the Street." He stopped humming mid-chorus. "Slide down to the floor. Now." He focused on the rearview mirror.

Ian slid to the floor.

"More."

He ducked his head and wedged himself into the foot box.

The doctor threw a blanket over him. "Stay still and don't breathe a word."

Under the blanket, the air from the heater grew stifling. Sweat dampened Ian's shirt.

Dink-dink, dink-dink. The car's blinkers. A slow turn and stop on the side of the road.

The whuh-whuh-whuh of a window crank was followed by a whistle of wind.

A moment later, an unfamiliar voice said, "Good morning, doctor. May I see your Identification Papers, driver's license, and registration, please."

"Good morning, officer." O'Brien sounded calm. "Did I do something wrong?"

"I'll be back in a moment."

"You're doing a good job," the doctor whispered. "Just a little while long—"

"Here, you go." The officer's voice grew closer. "You have a lot of stuff packed in here."

The doctor chuckled. "My wife says I carry everything including the kitchen sink. I say a vet can never be too prepared."

"Did you know you have a tail light out?"

"Do I?" The doctor sounded genuinely surprised.

"Left side."

"I'm on my way to help a dairy cow with mastitis. I'll get it fixed on my way back."

"A cow with what?"

"It's an infection of the teat that causes pus—"

"Okay, doctor. I get the idea. I'll let you go with a warning, but get that tail light fixed."

"Yes, sir, as soon as I take care of that cow."

It seemed like hours before O'Brien pulled the blanket off of Ian. "You can get up. The officer turned at the last intersection. I'll drive west for a while longer, to be sure, then go back to the place you had me park yesterday. Okay?"

Ian used the tail of his shirt to wipe his face, then studied the doctor's profile. "Why didn't you turn me in?"

He threw an are-you-crazy glance at Ian. "Why would I do that?"

"You'd earn more privileges from the Fellowship."

O'Brien snorted. "Like I want privileges from the Fellowship. I became a vet because I love animals, but that doesn't mean I don't love people, too. I don't care who believes what. Suffering is suffering and if I can do anything to relieve that, I will."

Ian's shoulders relaxed but he kept his smile inside. Junior had been right. The doctor was a good guy.

A half-hour later, O'Brien parked where he had yesterday but left the car running. "Ian, we need to talk."

"How do you know my name?"

"That's what the reporter called you yesterday. But I'm glad to know it really is. I've been looking for Henry Jr. When he didn't show up, I knew something was terribly wrong. The reporter said Henry and your parents were Taken. That you went into hiding. He didn't know what had happened to your other brothers and your sister." He tilted his head and gave Ian a compassionate look. "I know you think you can do this all on your own, but you need help. Your sister needs help."

Ian's stomach growled. "We appreciate your help—and your wife has been more than—" He glanced at the blanket covered pile of stuff in the back seat. The blankets moved. "What's that?" He drew back. His damp shirt mashed against the cold window.

O'Brien put his hand on Ian's shoulder. "Please, hear me out. Your brother would. I'll help your sister and keep your location a secret. All I ask is for you to give him five minutes."

The cold sliced through Ian, robbed him of the ability to breath, the ability to think, the ability to run.

"Ian, it's me." The familiar voice of the reporter, Claude Collins, set Ian's blood ablaze.

He whirled on O'Brien. "You've killed us. He'll Take us."

"What?" O'Brien shot a piercing look at Collins.

"No. I would never..." Collins sputtered.

Tiny flashes sparked in Ian's vision. "Liar!" He reached over the seat back, swung at Collins—missed. "You didn't want anyone to see you, but *I* saw you." His temples and chest pounded with the need to hurt Collins, to make him bleed. "Did you burn the symbol on the door before or after you Took my parents and Junior?"

Collins' mouth dropped open. His cheeks pinked. He closed his eyes and swallowed.

"You'd best answer the boy, Mr. Collins."

Collins locked eyes with Ian. "I came to get you—" He blew out a sharp breath. "Mr. Rice, the president of First Citizen's Bank, came on an earlier train." He pressed his lips together and shook his head. "The sign on your front door—I smelled charred wood and—panicked. I'm sorry. I should have looked for you. I did, later, but by then it was too late."

"Why should I believe you?" Ian huffed air in and out through clenched teeth.

"I guess you don't have much reason to believe me or anyone else."

"What are you doing here?"

"I've been following someone I suspected was a Fellowship rat—"

"The snitch you mentioned in the storage room at the paper?"

"Yeah. Anyway, I overheard him talking to someone about meeting at an abandoned barn. Then the doctor told me you were in a barn—"

"An abandoned—I didn't see you at the gas station...You listened to Monty when I called? You were at his house? You think Monty—?" Ian seethed. "Monty's not Fellowship—"

"He's Fellowship all right," Collins said. "He's been meeting with some Second Sphere agents at an old church on Elon road. I didn't figure you'd take my word for it. I have pictures." He offered Ian a small stack of photographs.

Ian's insides shook but his hand didn't show it when he took the photographs. In the first black and white photo, a man held the half-open rear passenger door of a dark Studebaker sedan parked in front of the abandoned church where Travis had been a prisoner. Ian's mouth went dry. He shuffled to the next photograph.

Ian's stomach dropped and his chest hollowed out. Monty stood in the door held by the man from the first photo. *There has to be a misunderstanding. Monty wouldn't.... Of course, they must have picked Monty up for questioning after we'd rescued Travis.*

He studied the photo closer. But the front of the church, not even the doors, had any sign of a gun battle. Not a single bullet hole. Queasy, Ian slid the next photograph out.

Monty stood on the top step, shook the hand of a tall man with military bearing who stood in the center of the open, double doors.

Pain twisted in Ian's chest. "No." Saying it out loud helped. "I don't believe it. Photos can be faked. I've known Monty my whole life. I'd know if he were Fellowship."

"I wouldn't want to believe it either," Collins said, "but those photographs are not fake."

Ian got out of the car. *I'm not taking any more of this bull hockey.*

O'Brien got out of the car. So did Collins.

"You have to believe me," Collins said.

"No, I don't." Ian glared at him. "I don't *have* to do anything." He locked eyes with the doctor. "I thought we could trust you." He turned and walked away. He didn't know where he was going. He couldn't go to the barn and he couldn't listen to Collins anymore.

"Ian, wait," O'Brien called. "Take this. Your sister needs her wound washed out again."

Ian stopped without turning around.

O'Brien came to his side, held out a small white sack and a

heavy grocery bag. "Wash it out then, put this ointment in the wound. It'll help clean it out while the bandage is on. If the redness and swelling aren't better by tomorrow, she needs a hospital."

Ian took the small white sack.

"This one's got food and water and soups for your sister. Take it. She's got to eat."

Ian hesitated, but the doctor was right. He took the bag of food.

"I'm sorry," O'Brien said in a low voice. "I don't know if he's telling the truth or not. He said this other boy is your best friend and that if you trust anyone, you'd trust him but that you shouldn't. I figured you needed to hear what he had to say so you could make up your own mind." He looked and sounded sincere.

"Monty saved my brother—saved *my* life—why would he do that if he's Fellowship?" Ian's voice cracked. "It isn't true. Collins is a liar. Don't let him follow me."

"He won't. I'll make sure of it."

Ian turned and walked toward the mountains.

He walked and walked. His memory played back all the times when as kids, Monty would disappear. He'd always say he had to do some charity something with his parents. He did work for charities. Ian had gone with him to the soup kitchen. They all knew Monty by name. Then he remembered how Monty had been able to meet him at the overlook in less than ten minutes. He couldn't have made that time from home.

Eventually, Ian made it back to the barn.

Kenny and Travis had a late lunch, early dinner of ham sandwiches and chortled with glee over chocolate bars.

Leslie took a few sips of the soup and looked less pale than she had. "Whatever you're worried about, you'll do the right thing. Things will work out." She gave him a wan smile and drifted back to sleep.

Ian took a bite of the ham sandwich and couldn't eat more. He didn't see how things would work out. *Collins wants me to turn on Monty. He wants me to remember all those times when Monty could have been doing things for the Fellowship. Why?* Ian's stomach lurched. *Monty's in trouble. They're going to go after Monty and his family.* He leaped to his feet. His sandwich hit the dirt.

"Where are you going?" Travis followed him to the other side of the wall of debris.

"I have to warn Monty," Ian said. "I—" Travis' expression made him abandon the lie he was going to tell. He put his hand on Travis' shoulder. "If I am not back by sundown tomorrow, you have to take Leslie and Kenny to the mountains and hide. Keep them safe for me."

Travis gasped. "You don't think you're ever coming back, do you?"

"I'll try, but going to our old neighborhood is risky."

"Monty's in danger?"

"Yeah."

"He saved us," Travis said. "Go. Help him. Sundown tomorrow I'll pack up. We'll start toward the cave the next day so you can find us."

Ian bumped fists with his brother, then hurried out of the barn.

CHAPTER 24

WITHOUT KENNY AND THE OTHERS, Ian traveled fast. He took a more direct route, parallel to but straighter than the road, and avoided the towns along the way. He walked non-stop for six and a half hours.

He slowed when he entered Monty's neighborhood. His breath made short steam clouds in the cold night air and his palms grew moist. Familiar places, homes he'd visited, appeared darker, more sinister than he'd ever known them to be. One of these former friends had betrayed his family. He didn't dare run into any of them. Only Monty had had his back.

He hunched his shoulders, pulled his hood tight around his face, and turned down the street behind Monty's.

The closer Ian got to Monty's house, the heavier his chest got. The back of his throat ached. He didn't want to find Monty's house like he'd found his own.

What if Monty *is* Fellowship rattled around inside of him no matter how many times he tried to banish it. He wiped sweat from his upper lip. *Collins is wrong. After everything Monty's done for us, he can't be the snitch.* Ian hated Collins for creating the niggling doubt that gnawed at him.

He hesitated a moment beside the old lady's garage. Every

window of her house was dark, as he'd expected. Still, it surprised him. Other people's lives had gone on. No one even noticed that his life had been destroyed. Resentment tasted like bile.

He cut through the old lady's yard and stood behind Monty's house. Most of the windows in Monty's dark and silent, two-story Georgia Colonial home stood open an inch. Monty's mom had a thing about fresh air keeping people healthy. Monty's bedroom window in the northeast corner was also open and dark.

Ian blew out a sharp breath and shook out his hands before he tossed a pebble at the window. It plinked against the glass. No light came on.

He tossed two more pebbles to be certain. Nothing. Monty always responded.

A funny tingle filled Ian's chest. He couldn't make himself go to the front door to see if—*No. Can't think that way.* There was only one other way to know.

The tree in the northeast corner had the same hand- and toe-holds, yet the climb wasn't the adventure it once had been.

He straddled the branch that reached over the roof and scooted toward the white iron balustrade that wreathed the widow's walk.

A practiced lean and swing landed him over the fence. He sidled along the railing to stand above Monty's window. He swiped his sweaty palms on his coat, then stepped over the fence. They'd had to stop using the drain pipe when they'd grown older, bigger.

He grabbed the bottom rail and lowered his body, stretched to his full length. Feet dangling, he caught the lip of Monty's window with his toes, landed his left, then his right foot on the window ledge. He reached with his right hand and seized the top of the window frame with his fingertips. Pressing himself against the brick, he inched his left hand down. He crouched on the windowsill a moment.

No sleeping Monty-shaped form lay on the bed and only the soft tick-tock of an alarm clock came from within. Ian slipped inside.

He flicked on the bedside lamp. The bed had the familiar patchwork quilt with multi-colored stars on it. Ian's pulse eased. *Monty's stuff is here. He hasn't been Taken.*

Monty always kept his room way neater than Ian's. From the maple dresser to the matching desk to the bedside table, uncluttered surfaces gleamed. No clothes were strewn about. Not a single drawer or closet door left ajar.

Under normal circumstances, Ian would make himself comfortable and wait for Monty to return from whatever event he was at, but nothing was normal for Ian anymore. *My being here could endanger Monty more. I'll leave a note.*

He crossed the room to Monty's desk. On the otherwise bare desktop, sat the camera-shaped wooden pencil holder Ian had made for him in shop class. It held a fountain pen, two pencils, and a long brass letter opener. Ian took one of the pencils.

Monty kept paper in one of the desk drawers, but Ian didn't remember which one. He pulled opened the top drawer. Inside were more pens and pencils, a pair of scissors, and packages of Bazooka chewing gum and black licorice.

The second drawer wouldn't open and neither would the third. Ian scanned the room. No loose paper anywhere. He had to get into one of those drawers.

Ian grabbed the letter opener. *Clink.* A metal-on-metal sound. He peered inside the pencil holder. A key.

The key slid into the second drawer's lock and turned easily. Neatly stacked inside the drawer were photographs and presentation folders. He gaped at the top photograph. It was of Claude Collins sharing a Fellowship-only sheltered bus stop with a woman whose brown skin color meant she was definitely not

Fellowship. *Why would Monty take this?* He knew it could get Collins and the woman arrested or worse.

Ian picked up the stack of photos and, careful to keep them in the same order, looked through them. There were photographs of Junior helping a black man inside Ma and Pop's store. Ian's throat ached. The next few photos held similar images of non-Fellowship types entering his parents' store. Ian looked closer. His mouth fell open. Collins and Ian's favorite history teacher, Mrs. Underhill, shook hands inside the store. *Pop never said he knew them.*

More photographs followed of Collins and Mrs. Underhill meeting in places no self-respecting Fellowship member would go. Ian set the photographs down on top of Monty's desk. Confusion swept over him. No Fellowship snitch would do those things. But Collins did.

All the photos had been taken from a distance. Not staged. Not grip and grins. And Monty took them all. Kept them all. Collins would say this proved Monty was Fellowship. Ian couldn't accept that. There had to be another reason.

Hands shaking, he took one of the presentation folders out of Monty's drawer and opened it.

———

This Certificate of Excellence
   Is rewarded to
   Montgomery Byrd Jones
   In recognition of invaluable service dedicated to preserving the Fellowship way of life through his identification of enemies of the state on this nineteenth day of November 1960.

———

Ian's chest had a planet-sized knot in it. Air wouldn't go in. Air wouldn't go out. The nineteenth. The day his parents and Henry Jr. were Taken.

He stumbled backward. The backs of his knees hit the bed. He gasped for air and couldn't tear his eyes from the folder on the desk. Monty, his buddy since grade school, the one guy on the planet with whom he shared everything—*had my parents and Henry Junior Taken?*

His temples throbbed with why, why, why? *Monty only pretended to be my friend? How did I not know? How could he...?* A surge of heat spread through Ian's veins and filled him with the overwhelming need to thrash, to beat, to pound Monty for what he'd done.

Oh dear God. Collins said Monty spoke to someone about meeting at an abandoned barn! His muscle twitched and shook. He struggled to steady himself enough to put the presentation folders back neatly with the photographs stacked on top. His hand shook so much it took two hands to get the key back into the lock and secure the drawer. He scanned the room once more before he turned out the bedside light and climbed out of the window.

Rage powered him down the tree and out of the neighborhood, it drove him faster, faster, faster.

CHAPTER 25

WILLIAMS SAT astride the horse and pulled his collar up, grateful for the warmth of the real sheepskin lining. His breath made short-lived frozen bubbles in the cold night air. After two twelve-hour days on horseback, searching dark and dank and dangerously decaying barns he had more than filled his lifetime quota. He had a sneaky feeling that Hobart had used them as a ruse. This was the tenth one, the last one, for today.

The breeze and crickets and other creatures created a lulling background hum. The way darkness put a sound dampening blanket in the countryside made him uneasy. He vastly preferred nights in the District. At least the full moon lit the sky enough tonight that they hadn't had to resort to flashlights yet.

Ahead of him, Fischer sat astride a horse with his dog's long leash tied to the saddle horn. Their routine had been to circle each barn. Thus far, the dog had been indifferent to every one.

Fischer raised his left arm, Xena raced back and forth, strained against her leash.

The dog has a scent. Williams sat straighter in the saddle, ignored how the motion rekindled the burn in his thighs and privates. He signaled everyone to fall back.

Fischer dismounted and gave the dog a hand signal. Head

down, tail high, the dog tracked a short zig-zag then headed straight toward the barn. She reached the barn door, tail wagging, and glanced back and forth at Fischer, then the door. Fischer pumped his right arm. *This is the place.*

A flush warmed Williams's neck and filled his chest. He signaled dismount and waved for Fischer to come close. Nickerson walked toward him as if he still had a horse between his legs.

Fischer and his dog joined them.

"Adler, you take the south side, Nickerson—the west," he whispered. "Fischer, you and the dog watch the back. If they are in there, we've got them."

"You can trust Xena. They're in there."

Williams grunted and painfully forced himself to take his usual stride toward the barn. Faint wood smoke scented the damp night air.

He had to admire the kids. There had been no tell-tale smoke visible. *Banks has never understood how woods-savvy these kids are.*

He signaled Adler, Fischer, and Nickerson and they disappeared around the corners of the barn. He waited long enough for them to get in position.

His pulse thrummed. The barn door stood ajar. It would allow a boy through but he couldn't squeeze through. Moving the door would likely make noises he couldn't control.

He raised his voice and powered it with authority. "Ian Hobart, the barn is surrounded. Come out peacefully."

A slight stirring noise came from inside.

His muscles tightened, primed for a chase. "I know you and your siblings are in there."

Still no answer.

Williams pushed the reluctant door open. It creaked and squealed. He sprang back to the shelter of the barn's wall.

Still nothing.

He's going to force a confrontation. Very well. Williams peered inside, then slipped into the barn and darted to his left.

The barn was dark and rank with rot and wood smoke. The moon shone through holes in the roof making the floor a patchwork of light and dark. *Another barn full of piles of debris.* The barn had no stalls. *It must have been a storage barn.*

He moved from dark patch to dark patch. *That's odd.* Debris at the far end of the barn formed a relatively straight line. *Like a defense wall.*

"Ian, don't make this harder than it has to be."

"We didn't do anything. Leave us alone."

His chest, his face, and his hands tingled and grew warmer. *A response. The second boy, Travis.* "I'm coming to you."

"Don't move." A rifle cocked.

Williams's pulse leaped. A bump near the midpoint of the wall wasn't a bump but a boy's head and the barrel of a rifle. *Where is the oldest?* "Put down the rifle, Travis. I'm here to help you." He oozed warmth and friendship through his voice.

"How do you know my name?"

"I've been looking for you, to help you. Come with me, I'll get you some food and a hot bath."

"We don't want your help." The boy's voice cracked.

I've got him. His middle son hated when his voice did that but it always signaled his son was about to cave. "We don't want to hurt you." He used the same soothing tone he used with his own children. "Where's Ian?"

A scraping, dragging sound came from behind the barrier. Williams couldn't identify what was being dragged. "Don't do anything stupid, Travis." He sidled to a darker patch of ground. "We've got you surrounded. Put down the rifle so no one gets hurt. You might hurt me, or one of my men, but you won't get away. And maybe one of you will get hurt."

The dragging sound continued.

"Adler," Williams called.

The click of a pistol being cocked rang out. Adler moved to the middle of what had once been a window, his pistol aimed toward the debris.

The dragging stopped for a moment, then started again.

"Nickerson."

A side door screeched open and a second pistol cocked.

The dragging stopped. Silence stretched for twenty, thirty seconds.

A dog growled.

Silence returned. Fifteen seconds.

"Okay," Travis said. "We give up, for now."

Williams had to smile at the "for now." So like his son. "Empty the rifle then toss it out toward me."

In the quiet the snick-click of the rifle's action being opened repeated seven times. Williams was glad he'd been cautious. The boy knew how to handle the gun.

A moment later the rifle hit the barn floor and slid toward him.

"Now, come on out."

The dragging sound happened again.

"Travis? What are you doing?"

"We're coming out. Don't shoot. I'm pulling my sister in her travois."

That's right. Monty said someone was injured. "We won't shoot. You can come out."

Slowly Travis came out of a hidden entrance, dragging the travois with the girl on it. The youngest boy trailed after them with his hands up in the air.

William's chest puffed up. He couldn't wait to get back to Banks with proof that he and his men were still good at their jobs.

CHAPTER 26

IAN SCRAMBLED THROUGH THE TREES, casting glances between openings in search of the barn. His breath caught and his stomach fell. He stopped short. The full moon glowed in the sky above the old red barn like a warning beacon. In the white moonlight, the doors stood wide open. The field surrounding the barn looked deserted. So did the barn, though he couldn't see into the black depths of it. The black depths held not one glimmer of firelight.

Travis said he wouldn't leave until in the morning. Ian's hands shook. His pulse filled his ears, his throat, his chest. Everything in his being screamed for him to run into the barn and find Travis and Kenny and Leslie. But if they had been captured, a Second Sphere agent, maybe more than one, would be watching the barn, waiting for his return.

Logic said run away. But he couldn't. He rubbed his mouth and chin. He had to know for certain. He studied the field and the derelict barn. To cross the field might mean he'd be captured or shot. He was not going to abandon his family, but he was not going to be an easy target either.

He crept across the ground, darted sometimes, crawled others. His body thrummed with energy that said run-run-run.

The stubs of cornstalks caught at his jacket and pulled as if to say don't go. He jerked his jacket free and circled to the back corner of the barn.

Kenny's bolt hole was unobstructed. Travis had moved the plywood, tried to escape. Chilled and breathless Ian studied the ground—no drag marks. *Travis wouldn't have left Leslie behind.* A slight stirring noise came from inside. Hope flickered. Ian crept to the edge and stuck his head through the hole. "Travis?" he whispered.

"Put your hands up."

Ian whirled and bolted for the trees.

Bang!

A surge of energy-fueled his legs and they pumped faster and faster.

The crashing, thrashing, pounding of pursuit came close behind him.

He plunged uphill, through the thickest of thickets. His world narrowed to the trees and bushes and plants in front of him and the noises behind him.

He ran until his legs cramped and he could not run another step. He grabbed his knotted calves and bent, waited for his pursuer. But the sounds behind him were gone. He didn't know when they'd stopped chasing him. He didn't know where he was. All he knew was the overwhelming ache in his chest. He gulped air that would never ease that ache.

He sank to his knees, buried his tearless face in his hands. He'd lost his entire family because he'd been too blind to see his friend was his foe. The ache swallowed him whole.

———

Ian turned his face away from the light, shivered, and reached for the blanket. "Go away, Travis," he mumbled sleepily and groped empty air. The sound of his own voice accompanied by the wind in the trees reminded him. He wasn't home in his bed. He had no blanket. Travis wasn't here. Neither was Leslie or Kenny. His teeth chattered. He squinted up at the sun. Its bright beams unobstructed by the bare branches of the trees provided little warmth.

Part of him insisted that he get up and move or he would die out here. He probably had hypothermia. Part of him said that was okay. This was his fate, to lie here and die alone. He tried to go back to sleep but sleep wouldn't come. He couldn't sleep because his toes ached with cold. Correction, only the toes on his right foot ached like that. He sat up and gaped at his muddy, shoeless and sockless right foot. Mud crusted halfway up to the knees of his pant legs.

He didn't remember stepping in any mud, much less losing his sock and shoe. He sighed and lay back down. *I left them alone. I knew Travis couldn't pull the travois fast enough to save them. I should have stayed. I should have protected them. I don't deserve to die of hypothermia. I should have been Taken.*

The ache in his chest changed to something diamond hard and filled with the need to punish. Not just punish but destroy in the most excruciating way. The need to repay pain with greater pain.

But he had nothing—worse, he had no one. Acting alone, his chances of survival, of finding and free Leslie, Travis, and Kenny if they were still alive, were nonexistent.

Monty's photos flashed through his memory. Each image drove the bite of Monty's dirty, double-crossing lies deeper.

The images burned through his mind. They stoked a fire so hot it seared away the ache.

The idea that Mrs. Underhill and Collins were anti-Fellowship circled round and round in his head. Ian couldn't decide if they were rebels or not, but he needed a weapon and some information. Both of them were experts at finding information. And if that's all they could give him, that would be enough. He'd fight the Second Sphere—the whole darned Fellowship—on his own, no matter the odds. Surviving didn't matter anymore. Making Monty and the Fellowship pay, that was what mattered.

Ian shielded his eyes and looked up. The sun was two fingers west of overhead. That meant Mrs. Underhill would be in school, teaching. Ian certainly couldn't go to Collins at the newspaper. But there was one person he could go to. The one person he knew who had no connection to Monty. He stood and dusted off the dead leaves that stuck to his clothes, then trotted toward Glasgow, determined he'd make it there before the vet's clinic closed for the day.

CHAPTER 27

IAN PACED the concrete floor in the center of the barn in borrowed shoes and socks. This was the cleanest barn he'd ever seen even with four of its six stalls filled with sick animals. He couldn't believe that all he had accomplished so far was to exchange one barn for another.

Sweat saturated his shirt under his arms, down his chest and back. He'd shed his jacket more than an hour ago. The energy that had driven him here, the sustenance of the two sandwiches the doctor had shared with him, left. He sank onto a wood bench against the wall in the tack room. The tack room held shelves and hooks with an assortment of animal care items. Heavy wool blankets sat on a shelf below the ropes and bridles and halters hanging on the wall. He snorted. Here he sat, too warm and with more blankets than he and his siblings had seen in weeks. Blankets they had desperately needed. The irony burned his stomach. He didn't need blankets now. The diamond-hard thing that had grown inside him said all he needed now was to make Monty pay.

The doctor had called Collins a couple of hours ago. Ian feared he had made a mistake. Not in trusting the doctor. The doctor had proven himself, but maybe Collins was like Monty. Maybe Collins had called the Second Sphere. But if he had, wouldn't the SS have already come? Ian's eyes burned. He closed them for a minute.

The noise of barn doors sliding startled him awake. He scrambled to his feet and peered out of the tack room.

"Ian?" The doctor waited with his back to the closed doors. Claude Collins stood next to the doctor, his eyes searching the barn around him.

Ian released the breath he held and stepped into the main part of the barn.

Claude Collins nodded at him.

He nodded back. Now that Collins was here, Ian didn't know what to say. Somehow the words, 'I'm sorry I thought you had my family killed,' didn't want to come out of his mouth. "Did the doctor tell you—"

"That your sister and brothers were captured by the Second Sphere? Yes. I would have been here earlier, but I did a little investigating." Collins ran a hand through his hair. "I'm afraid it's not good news."

The diamond hard rock inside Ian prepared him.

"We're pretty sure they're in that abandoned church where..."

Unexpected, the news hit him like a two-by-four. Something in his chest fluttered. "They're alive?"

"The amount of food and water being taken into the church now suggests they are."

"You haven't seen them?" Ian's voice fell, hard like his insides.

"No," Collins leveled a concerned look at him, "but—"

He stiffened. "But what?"

"There's a sign on the door. It's addressed to you."

Fists balled at his sides, he glared at Collins. "What does it say?"

Collins and the doctor exchanged glances. The doctor

nodded a go-on.

"What does it say?" More forcefully.

"Ian, they're here. Give up and they'll survive." Collins gave him a sympathetic look.

He gulped one big breath after another. The diamond inside him refused to soften, refused to believe. "They lie." He forced the words out as fast as he could. "They're already dead. Right?"

Collins didn't pull back, didn't flinch. "We're certain they're alive. Otherwise, the supplies wouldn't be going into that church. We want to help you rescue them."

The possibility gutted him then his insides hardened again. He looked Collins square in the eye. "If they're alive, I have to do more than rescue them. I have to make sure they are safe—forever." He didn't say how he'd like to make them safe. How he'd like to make Monty pay for a lifetime of lies.

"We can help with that, too," Collins said. "But we need something from you, Ian."

He cocked his head at Collins. *Of course, you do.*

"We need you to be calm and cool-headed and follow orders."

He shook his head. Calm and cool-headed belonged somewhere else. Not here. Not now. And as for following orders— forget that nonsense. "Never mind. I'll figure my own stuff out. I've done okay so far."

"Really?" Collins said. "You did pretty well for a while, but it wasn't easy, was it? And your sister got hurt. And you didn't have enough to eat, enough clothes, or a place to go—And now your brothers and sister are prisoners of the Second Sphere and will be shipped to re-education tomorrow."

"Well, I'm sorry, I didn't plan on my parents being Taken. On the four of us being left with *nothing* and no one to count on."

"Look. I understand how you feel."

Ian gaped at him. "You do? You had your parents Taken? You

brothers and sister captured? Nothing left to your name? All because of a—"

"A friend who betrayed you? No, you're right," Collins said. "I don't know exactly what you're going through. But I know if it were me, I'd want to beat the crap out of someone. And because I'm not you, I know if you go off half-cocked and do something stupid, your brothers and sister will pay for it tomorrow and for the rest of their lives."

Ian inhaled ready to argue, then stopped. He'd heard stories of what happened in re-education centers. Beatings and torture and there were rumors that six out of ten people who went into re-education died. The rumors had disturbed him before, now they chilled him more than the iciest river.

He blew out a long breath. His shaking had stopped. He didn't know when. Breathing was easier, too. That diamond inside him had settled into place. And the diamond-hard place inside cooled him, told him he could do whatever it took. He was not going to let Leslie, Travis or Kenny spend one day in re-education. He squared his shoulders and met Collins' eyes. "Tell me what to do."

CHAPTER 28

IN A ROADSIDE MOTEL outside of Snowden, Ian stood in a room with a kitchenette flabbergasted that his high school history teacher cooked smoke bombs. He couldn't reconcile the tiny woman in her high-necked blouse, pleated skirt, and cats-eye glasses with the rebel at the stove. He glanced from the brown sludge that bubbled in the skillet to the pile of aluminum foil "boats" on the table and back again.

Quick and efficient, Mrs. Underhill added more ingredients and stirred them into the gooey mixture. She knew exactly when to remove it from the stove and scrape it into one of the aluminum boats.

She must have made hundreds of smoke bombs. I wonder if she makes real bombs, too.

Behind them, Mr. Collins sat at the table. He took the still warm goo and placed fuses in the middle of it. Then, he molded the gunk into a large, blunt bullet shape and sealed the foil around it. Then he set the smoke bombs aside to cool.

He glanced up, noticed Ian watched him. "We've experimented with this particular waxed rope." He folded foil around the next smoke bomb. "Once this is lit it's about one minute to detonation."

Ian stiffened. "It explodes?"

Collins looked up, chagrined. "There's no danger to your brothers and sister. It causes a bang, a pop really, and a flash when the contents catch fire. It spews thick smoke immediately." He held up a cooled, aluminum foil smoke bomb. "One of these would fill this room with smoke in less than sixty seconds."

Ian gawked at Collins, feature reporter and rebel, then at Mrs. Underhill, history teacher and rebel. Hs world had gone bonkers. He couldn't resolve what he'd once thought with what he now knew. And these two were plotting against Second Sphere agents to help him rescue his brothers and sister. He wiped his sweaty hands on the clean jeans Mrs. Underhill had given him.

"—and while we're doing that, what are you doing?" Mrs. Underhill stared at Ian and waited.

Uh, oh. "I'm sorry, what did you say?"

"We only have a few hours to prepare. It's vital that you focus."

Ian chafed at the lecturing tone. "Why can't we distract them like Monty did?"

"Three reasons. One, they're prepared for that kind of assault at the church now. Two, what if your brothers and sister are in the front of the church this time and one of them got shot? And three, what if they shoot you?"

Monty knew exactly where Travis was when he was shooting. He could have turned me in then. But he didn't. Heck, he could have turned us in instead of driving us up to Quarry Road. It doesn't make sense. I need answers. "What if I hold Monty hostage?"

Mrs. Underhill turned off the stove and with the skillet in hand, gave Ian a frank look. "What makes you think they consider Monty a valuable asset?"

In a perverse way, that idea pleased Ian. "Okay. I call him at eight." *Maybe I'll call a little early. A few minutes alone with him and I'll get my answers.* "I tell him I need his help 'cause they captured Leslie, Travis, and Kenny."

"Not with that tone of voice. Come on, Ian. You have to say it like you mean it. Your sister and brothers—all of our lives—depend on you convincing Monty you still trust him."

Ian unclenched his fists. "I call on the Handie Talkie." Collins had given him fresh batteries. "I'm desperate. I can't risk being seen, so we'll meet at the overlook again."

"Keep working on that."

Collins stood and stretched. "What if he comes with company?"

He blinked at Collins, then Mrs. Underhill. "That's what we're hoping for, isn't it?"

Mrs. Underhill peered at him over the tops of her glasses. "Yes. But please, tell us what you're going to do."

"I'll be in the woods. I can see anyone coming to the overlook parking lot, so I'll be prepared." Ian focused on the row of foil-wrapped bombs on the table so he didn't have to lie to Mrs. Underhill's face.

"If Monty has company, I lead them through the woods. I'll use a smoke bomb to slow them down then, after fifteen minutes, I surrender." It wasn't exactly a lie. He'd use the smoke bomb all right. He'd use it to get Monty alone for fifteen minutes.

Mrs. Underhill filled the sink with hot water.

"They could take you somewhere other than back to the church." Collins crossed to the window and peered out between the edges of curtains.

Ian's insides hardened. "If they do, it gives you guys more time with less resistance at the church." And he'd show the Second Sphere resistance until his last breath.

"Yes, it does." Collins turned and met Ian's eyes. "But we can't come looking for you until your brothers and sister are safe at the old lady's cabin." They wouldn't give him her name until he was on the way there. Just in case...

"I know." He stuck his hands deep inside his pockets so no one could see how badly they shook.

Mrs. Underhill dried the clean skillet and packed it into her suitcase. Then she and Collins packed the now-cooled smoke bombs into three separate paper lunch sacks.

Collins handed him a heavy lunch sack. "Three smoke bombs, a no-fail candle lighter, a thermos of water, and my promise that we'll be there."

A flush raced up Ian's neck, tingled the backs of his ears. The paper bag crinkled with every tremble of his hands. He held it close to his chest, stilling his hands for the moment.

"Once you let them catch you and they take you inside the church. Then what?"

If— His tense muscles ached. "I insist they show me that Leslie, Travis, and Kenny are alive."

"It's imperative that you know where they are within the first five minutes—*before* we lob a smoke bomb inside."

He bit his lower lip. *Lecturing is Mrs. Underhill's teacher habit. She isn't my enemy.* He blew out his breath and relaxed his shoulders.

"After that?" Collins crossed the room.

"I turn cooperative—until you throw the smoke bomb inside."

"The Alpha and Beta teams will smash through windows on both sides of the building at the same time." Collins turned and faced him again. "Wait for the smoke bomb. It'll come from the last window on the north side."

"I drop to the floor, wet my kerchief if I can, and cover my nose and mouth, and crawl straight to Leslie and the boys."

"You have just a minute or two before the open window will clear the room enough that the agents can see you. I'll be—"

"At the last window on the south side. I know," Ian said. "I'll bring Leslie to you."

"Others will be there to help your brothers. Follow them out —fast."

"I will."

"As soon as you're outside, we'll open fire to cover you. Stay low but run like hell to the trees. We'll meet at the extraction point. If you're not there in fifteen minutes we move on. We'll be at the secondary extraction point at midnight."

A shiver ran up Ian's spine. He clamped his teeth together and nodded once.

Mrs. Underhill picked up her suitcase. She held a hand out to Ian.

Her hand was warm, her grip snug and sure. "Good luck."

She shook with Collins, then slipped out the door.

Collins watched out the window. "You might as well sit. We're going to be here a little while."

Ian pulled the wooden chair from the desk, straddled it facing the back of the chair.

A car engine started, then pulled away and faded into the distance.

Collins turned to Ian. "There's—uh—something you might want to know."

"Huh?"

"Remember that article you wrote?"

Ian stiffened, gripped the back of the chair tight. "Yeah."

"I did a little digging. You've got good instincts. Alan Baker, the Fellowship leader you followed, is corrupt all right."

Ian's throat clamped shut. He closed his eyes.

"The dump is a cover for his loan shark business. The truck drivers pick up payments and threaten anyone who doesn't pay." A pained expression settled on Collins's face. "He would never report you or your family to the Fellowship. They might look too closely at what he's doing." He cleared his throat. "I—uh—thought you'd want to know."

Ian gulped several breaths before he could speak. "Yeah. Good to know." His voice shook. It helped to know he wasn't the cause of what had happened to his family. He rested his chin on his hands. Yet, it didn't help. His parents and Junior were still gone and Leslie and the boys were still prisoners.

The silence between them stretched into minutes.

Collins stood. "In ten minutes, Doctor O'Brien will come for you." He raised a hand, stopped Ian's unspoken protest. "He'll drive you to a point about a mile past the overlook. Hike back to the overlook and make your call at eight o'clock sharp."

They shook hands and Mr. Collins left.

Ian peered out the window through the narrow gap between the curtains.

Ten minutes crawled one excruciating second at a time.

Finally, the dark blue Power Wagon parked outside the motel room. Ian picked up the lunch bag and stepped outside. His glance swept the otherwise empty parking lot and the line of cheap motel rooms.

He went straight to the car, climbed into the passenger seat.

The doctor backed out and turned onto the highway.

Trees zipped past.

Dr. O'Brien drove in silence for a few minutes before he spoke. "I'll be waiting for your sister at the cabin."

Startled, Ian whipped around to stare. "Mrs. Underhill told me that already." Then it hit him. He snorted. "Mrs. Underhill had you pick me up so you could talk to me. Give me a pep talk or something, right?"

"Something like that."

Ian braced himself for another lecture. "So say your piece."

O'Brien kept his eyes forward but smiled a little. "Ian, if I were you, I'd be so full of every emotion I don't think I would be able to function."

Ian cocked his head. "But..." He couldn't keep the sarcasm from his voice.

"But nothing. You are an incredibly strong and honorable young man who has been through more in the last few weeks than most people experience in a lifetime. I wanted you to know that. You are a survivor—no matter what life throws at you—you are an honorable man and a survivor, the kind of man the rebellion needs." He sounded sincere.

Ian blinked and blinked again. *Was that a dig or an offer?*

O'Brien focused on the road.

Ian stared at the trees without seeing them. No one except Ma and Pop had talked to him that way before. He squeezed his lower lip between his thumb and forefinger and tried to figure out what that meant.

The dink-dink of the car's blinker warned him.

"Are you ready?"

He glanced at his wristwatch. Seven-fifty. He was as ready as he knew how to be. The car stopped, he exited and melted into the trees.

CHAPTER 29

WILLIAMS SCANNED the gravel drive leading to the church. The crunch-crunch-crunch of Adler's and the Major's footsteps distracted him. He re-focused. *We have the perfect bait. Hobart is all but mine. He probably won't come by road, but better be prepared.*

Adler drew his hand above the invisible-in-the-dark cord eight inches off the ground. "This is one of our perimeter warning devices."

"Excellent." Banks turned to Williams. "You should have employed his talents sooner."

His jaw muscles ached. He kept his gaze on the tripwire, away from Banks. It didn't help one's career to let one's superiors know how much you loathed them. Not that he'd have a career much longer if Banks had his way.

"When the oldest Hobart trips it, it'll pull the paracord loose from this clothespin." Adler followed the cord to the tree where he'd nailed the clothespin. "These screw heads will touch and activate the radio." One red and one black coated wire led to a box which Adler opened and revealed the insides of a Handie Talkie. "It sends a signal to us that our radio picks up as a buzz."

Even knowing where the cord was, Williams could barely

make it out. *We should have more men. If I had more men, I'd station one here ready to capture Hobart when he tripped the signal instead of hoping he actually trips the tripwire.*

"Tripwires cover the entire perimeter." Adler returned to the road, stood between Williams and Banks. "The others trigger a doorbell from the north, a longer buzz from the east, and a shorter buzz from the west."

Banks rubbed his hands together. "Good, very good." Banks turned to Monty. "Our plan depends upon him reaching out to you. You're certain he'll call you?"

Monty's white teeth flashed in a too-confident smile. "He's got no one and nothing else. Of course, he'll call."

"Our wiretap on Mr. Jones' telephone?" Banks snubbed Williams, directed his question to Adler.

Williams stepped between them. "It's operational." Years of training made his voice devoid of the fire that surged in his veins. The fire that strained for release. "Nickerson is monitoring it now. They alternate watch every two hours at the top of the hour. Adler will relieve him soon."

"Excellent, then Adler will remain on duty until Mr. Jones gets the call." Banks walked back toward the church, his syco-phants trailed after him.

Williams sucked in a breath. Another obstacle. "Then— Adler will crouch in the back seat while young Monty drives out to meet Hobart."

Monty stiffened at the word, "young."

Williams counted that a victory and followed the others inside. "When Hobart is in the car and the car is in motion, Adler will arrest him."

"We'll get our man, won't we, Mr. Jones?" Banks gave Monty an approving nod then breezed through the open doors of the church.

Williams suppressed his urge to roll his eyes. At least, he'd won the argument to prepare the sanctuary. A barricade of pews and the altar table stood in the foyer before the sanctuary's double doors. That would be Nickerson's position now.

Banks rounded the barricade and waited for Adler to open the doors. Adler moved to enter after Banks, before Williams.

Williams pushed through the doorway before Adler, his back stone stiff. The older Hobart boy wasn't the only one walking into a trap.

His mind cycled various plans but so far none of his ideas took out both of his enemies at once. Before either one of them could arrange for him to be Taken.

The cold of the dark sanctuary knifed through his coat. They'd blocked all the windows in the church with plywood, but in the sanctuary each of the boards had weapon slots cut into them. The wind whistled through the slots.

Banks and Monty thought they knew the oldest Hobart. But while Hobart would attempt to recover his family, he would not do it the same way he'd done before.

The oldest Hobart boy was at least as smart as any of the clever opponents Williams had faced in the past. Hobart's inexperience, his emotional attachment to his siblings—that was what they should target.

Williams clenched his fists and struggled to keep from panting like a rabid dog. Banks had overruled him. Instead of taking the children to Redemption, and going after Hobart in a no-holds-barred way, Banks determined they'd tease Hobart. The children sat in the same anteroom in which the middle Hobart boy had been held before he was rescued. Williams had argued that they should be in a different room, but Banks argued that the sanctuary was more defendable. *It would be if I had more men, trustworthy men.*

To defy Banks would be a death sentence. To follow his orders and fail, as Williams strongly suspected would happen, also carried a sentence of death. *Whatever I do must be unsuspected, spontaneous, and lethal.*

He breathed in the crisp pine-scented air and silently asked the Lord to deliver the older boy to him, to grant his survival, and to allow him to return home to his family.

CHAPTER 30

IAN MADE another loop around the trees behind the overlook's parking lot. The purr of a car drew close. It approached from the south like Monty would. The burn in Ian's chest intensified and every muscle ratcheted tighter and tighter.

Headlights appeared and disappeared as the vehicle made its way over the undulations of the road. Finally, the sedan turned into the parking lot and passed under the lone streetlight. *It* was *Monty.* The car stopped in the darkest corner of the parking lot. Ian tasted dust, couldn't swallow.

Monty climbed out of the car, stood by the open door, and scanned the overlook. He walked around to the front of the car and glanced around again.

Ian balled his fists and shot searing beams of hate at Monty.

Monty stood in front of his car and did a slow three-sixty.

The need to pummel, pound, pulverize Monty drove Ian three steps forward. He ground his teeth and trembled with the effort to stop. *Must make him wait. Give Collins and the others time to reconnoiter the church.*

Monty walked into the grass and did another turn. "Ian? Where are you?"

Ian counted seconds. At sixty, he unclenched his fists and

stepped out of the trees. "Monty." His voice sounded hard, unnatural, even to him.

Monty crossed over to him, wrapped him in a hug, and pounded his back. "Man, it's good to see you. I was afraid…" Monty pulled back, searched his face. "We'll get Leslie, Travis, and Kenny. Those Second Sphere agents won't expect us to hit them again."

Ian forced a smile. "You have a plan?"

"Yeah, get in the car, we'll talk on the way." Monty walked back toward the car.

Ian didn't follow him. "We need to figure out the plan here. Then, we can leap into action the moment we arrive."

Monty faced him, his head tilted and his eyebrows lowered. "If we talk on the way, we get there sooner." He spoke soft and slow.

"Talk to me here, Monty." Too harsh. Ian forced another smile. At least one Second Sphere agent should be here by now. He scanned the tree line across the road and behind him.

Eyes fixed on Ian, Monty adjusted his stance, planted his feet. "What's wrong?"

He clenched his fists and took a menacing step toward his Judas. "My parents and Junior are dead. My sister's badly hurt. She and my brothers have been arrested. And the Second Sphere wants me dead. What do you *think* is wrong?"

"Okay, okay." Monty made calm-down motions with his hands and took two steps back. "We can talk here for a minute."

Ian forced his hands to unclench. The muscles ached to tighten again. He ran a hand through his hair and calmed himself. "So how do you think we should go in this time?"

"Well, last time worked pretty well except for the get-away."

"Except they took the rifle along with Travis and the others."

"I thought of that. There's another weapon in the trunk." He smirked. "I think we should stick together this time. That way I can give you cover the whole time."

Ian gave a quiet snort. "So we walk in the front door with your gun blazing?"

A puzzled look crossed Monty's face again. "You have something different in mind?"

"What if we make smoke bombs—" *Crap! That was the wrong thing to say.* "—or set fire to the front of the building?"

Monty frowned and appeared to think about it for a moment. "I think both of those could end up causing us problems—Smoke bombs would make us unable to see, too. And a fire could block the door or go through that old building so fast we couldn't get to your sister and brothers."

Ian pretended to consider what Monty said, then nodded. "You're right. Okay, so we go in with you providing cover. We going to drive up to the church itself?"

Monty shook his head. "They'd hear us coming and have too much time to prepare. But we should park closer this time. Get there faster."

"Right." Still no Second Sphere agents in sight. He couldn't delay for fifteen minutes if they didn't show up and chase him. *I have Monty alone right now. I could demand answers...*

"You ready to go, now?" Monty watched him carefully.

Undecided, Ian hesitated.

"How did you say Leslie got hurt?" Monty asked. "Do we need to take her to a doctor?"

Ian's cheeks burned. "She fell." It took him several moments to regain control. He swallowed hard, the sandpaper of his throat made him want to grab his neck but he didn't. "Let's go get her and Travis, and Kenny."

Monty walked alongside him, watching him all the way to the car.

A glance revealed the empty back seat. He climbed into the

front. This isn't how it was supposed to go pounded through his head and his blood.

Monty pulled out of the parking lot and focused all his concentration on the drive. He no longer side-eyed Ian or even glanced Ian's way.

The nearer they got to the church the more Ian had to force himself to sit still and not glare at the traitor.

Pop. The sound came from the back seat. He turned and at the same time, the back seat folded forward and a Second Sphere agent in the trunk pointed a gun at him.

"In the name of the Fellowship, Ian Henry Hobart, you will surrender."

Icy tendrils twined around Ian from his brain to his toes.

Monty whipped his head around. His eyebrows raised and his mouth made an "oh" shape. "Where did you come from?"

Ian gaped at him, not fooled for a second. Certainty snapped into place and a flush of heat raced from his center to his fingers and toes. It boiled away the ice.

"You, driver. Shut up and pull over." The gun waved toward Monty for a half-second then targeted Ian again.

Monty pulled onto the shoulder, put the car in park, and turned off the engine.

"How did you—"

"Shut up, Monty." Ian's taut throat gave his words flat-out hostility.

"Ian, I—"

"You think I'm a fool?" Guttural, his voice vibrated with venom.

"What are—"

"No more pretending, Monty." Liquid fire rushed through his veins. The effort not to launch a fist at Monty's jaw sent a violent tremor through him.

"Pretending?"

"I was in your room. I saw the photographs. The *certificates*—" A shudder choked off the rest of his words.

Something dark rippled across Monty's face, changed his expression from concern to haughty self-satisfaction. "You didn't turn your parents in, so I had to."

"You ate at our table, played Scrabble with Junior, and got Christmas presents from my parents. They considered you family." Ian glared at Monty but kept the gun in the edges of his vision.

"Family doesn't put family at risk by defying the Fellowship."

"True religion doesn't ask its members to betray anyone. And as sure as your Aunt Sally, religion doesn't make family kill one another."

"If you were a believer, you'd understand."

"If you're a believer, why didn't you turn us in instead of driving us up to Quarry Road?"

Monty's eyes darted to the agent in the backseat, then settled back on Ian. "I'd gotten one award for turning in your parents." His smile made Ian sick. "Another award would have earned me another level as a Second Sphere cadet."

The lava in Ian's veins flooded his vision, blinded him. He drew back a fist.

"Don't." The man in the backseat had crawled out of the trunk. He touched the cold gun barrel to Ian's temple.

Ian turned statue. His pulse jumped in his neck.

"Slow and easy, put your hand in your lap."

Ian stayed frozen. Part of him begged, cried, screamed for him to throw that punch. A remote voice in his head said to be calm. *Wait. For Leslie and Travis and Kenny. Bide your time.*

"Now." The gun barrel pressed a hole in his temple.

Ian made a show of straightening his fingers, splaying them, then lowered his hand to his lap. His fingers clawed his pant leg, contracted into a fist again. He tightened his fingers, then forced them to loosen and tighten again. The tiny action didn't release the fury trapped inside him.

"Take us to headquarters," the man in the backseat said.

"My pleasure." Monty started the engine, pulled out onto the road.

They rode in silence. Monty had a smug smile on his face. Ian had a pistol barrel pressed to his pulsing temple.

CHAPTER 31

WILLIAMS HAD difficulty reading his watch in the dimly lit sanctuary. He stuck his wrist in front of the slot in the plywood-covered window. Faint moonlight made the watch face glow. Nine o'clock. *And no word from Adler yet.*

Though he sat calm and still, he had internal fidgets worse than he'd had on the night of his eldest son's first date. Except his son's date had been a soft-spoken daughter of an upstanding Fellowship member, not a duplicitous sleeper snitch.

At least the kids in the anteroom next to him had settled down. The youngest had wailed for the better part of an hour after their arrival. The middle brother said the boy was afraid of the dark. Williams had relented and allowed them a flashlight and it had grown blessedly quiet after that.

He sat in the north end of the sanctuary, positioned to take advantage of the slot in the plywood if things didn't go as planned. He'd be surprised if dirty-dealing Monty delivered the oldest Hobart boy as promised. A sleeper couldn't be trusted.

Banks sat across the room from him and Nickerson held his position in the foyer.

Shh. Shh. The radio. "We're en route." *Adler. At last.* "The package is in hand. I say again. The package is in hand."

Williams wriggled his neck, released a tiny bit of tension. He didn't move from his position, neither did the others. They'd all had experience with last-minute disruptions in planned events. He prayed that this time there were no surprises.

Buzz. The driveway tripwire. Still, Williams didn't move. A few moments later, the roar of a car engine grew near, stopped in front of the building. Car doors clunked.

Williams took a deep breath of moist, earthy air. He imagined the sweet homecoming greetings he would get from his wife and children.

Footsteps clomped up the steps and into the foyer.

"Halt." Nickerson performed his duty with authority. Feet shuffled on the wood floors.

Williams pictured the pat-down Nickerson gave Hobart. Any minute now he would finally meet this adversary, this young man who had challenged and shamed him.

The doors to the sanctuary opened. Monty strutted in, a smirk on his face. He stepped to the side and Hobart walked in, followed closely by Adler and Nickerson.

Hobart settled into a natural parade rest stance. His hair, overlong and tangled, fell into his eyes. His eyes searched the room.

Banks strode across the room, stopped an arm's length away. "Mr. Ian Hobart, I presume."

Williams's internal alarms sent pinpricks down his spine. He rose slowly, assessed the young man. Hobart stood quietly, hands behind his back, and stared straight ahead. *No, not straight.* He fixed his stare on the door to the anteroom. *That was as it should be but....*

"You should have been in Redemption weeks ago. Why did you resist? Did you have help from the rebels?"

Hobart glanced at Banks, then returned his gaze to the anteroom door. "I won't talk until I see my sister and brothers."

Banks laughed. "Young man, you are not in a position to make demands. You will cooperate or you will never see your family again."

Hobart's gaze remained fixed on the anteroom door.

"Who helped you?"

No answer.

Oh, for crying out loud. Williams strode to the anteroom door and banged on it. "Each of you, say your names loudly."

"Leslie can't talk loud."

"Very well. Next."

"Travis."

"Kenny."

Hobart visibly relaxed.

He's too relaxed...something's off...

"You've made a mess of things, young man." Banks paced in front of him. "Had you gone to Redemption you would have..."

Williams had to admire the boy. He didn't react, maintained his parade rest posture, unmindful of his unzipped, green tweed coat and too-big jeans, cinched tight at the waist with a leather belt.

That was it! His person and his clothes were cleaner than they should be. The other children had obviously been living in the woods. *Why and how did he get cleaned up?* Williams took two strides forward.

A short buzz came from the radio—someone triggered the west—the doorbell rang and a long buzz sounded. Williams whirled toward the anteroom.

Something shiny flew through the slot in the south window. It thunked and rolled along the floor.

He turned and squinted at it.

Thwack! It flared and spewed thick gray smoke that billowed, flowed across the room.

"Secure Hobart!" His shout ended in a fit of coughing.

CHAPTER 32

THE FIRST SMOKE bomb arced through the slot in the sanctuary window and landed on the floor. Ian dropped to his knees. His driving need to punch and pound transformed into a pulse-pounding need to get to his siblings. The second and third foil-wrapped missiles thudded to the floor through other window slots and detonated. Smoke filled the room faster than he'd thought possible.

He crawled away from Monty and the agents who'd brought him into the sanctuary. They'd taken the water bottle away, but he still had the kerchief. He tied it around his head, covering his mouth but the dry kerchief couldn't stop the thick smoke. A dry, wracking cough shook him.

Tears streamed from his eyes and his lungs screamed for air. Lips pressed tight, he tried to cough quietly and crawled toward the anteroom. His skin twitched with the expectation of an explosion of gunfire, but it didn't come.

Over the hacking coughs and the hiss of the smoke bombs, screams erupted from the anteroom.

"Fire! Let us out! Fire!" Panic made Travis's voice strident.

He couldn't yell and reassure Travis, he'd give his position away. He crawled faster.

Someone grabbed his ankles. He fell flat, rolled and used his free leg to give a mighty kick. One hand let go, the other didn't. His second kick only found air. He twisted the opposite direction and kicked again, connected with a solid body part. Pain jolted his ankle and knee. The hand let go.

Ian couldn't see. Every breath sent knives through his throat and lungs. He coughed so hard he was grateful he hadn't eaten recently. Army crawling, uncertain of his position, he bumped his head on a flat vertical surface.

Please let it be the anteroom door. He rose to his knees and groped the surface. It was a wall. *Crap!*

He slid his hand along the wall and found a corner, and then the door. A chair had been jammed against the doorknob. He yanked it free. The doorknob wouldn't budge.

Travis had stopped yelling, but convulsive coughing came from inside.

He leaned against the door and tried to speak in a normal voice. "Travis?" His raw throat strangled the word.

"Ian! Get us out of here!" Someone pounded on the door from the other side.

"Don't let us burn!"

"It's not a fire," he said. "Get away from the door—" His shout ended in a coughing spasm. He took a step back, focused as well as he could on the spot four inches away from the doorknob, and kicked with everything he had.

Crack! Wood splintered and the door sprang open.

In an instant, arms wrapped around his waist and chest. He gave Travis and Kenny a quick hug but didn't have time to indulge in reunion joy. "Where's Leslie?"

"Here." Travis pulled him to where Leslie lay on a blanket on the ground.

"Leslie?" His voice sounded low and croaky. "We're getting out of here. I'll carry you."

Crashing, splintering sounds came from the sanctuary. He whirled toward the sound. *I'm late! They're breaching the window already.*

He swiveled back to Leslie. "Sorry, we've got to go!" He lifted her into a fireman's carry over his shoulder. "Travis, grab Kenny with one hand and my belt with the other. Do it now! Don't let go of Kenny. Single file. Let's go!"

"Got him." Travis grabbed his belt.

Ian took shallow breaths and tried not to cough. A quick shuffle got them through the door.

In the sanctuary, the last window to his left had been breached. A man's shadow filled the window. *Collins?* Ian blinked to clear his vision. He still couldn't tell. He had to trust it was.

"Give her to me." Collins's voice was muffled.

Ian bent forward, Leslie's weight lifted away. He reached behind him. "Kenny?"

Coughing uncontrollably, Kenny stumbled into him.

He lifted Kenny up and out into a pair of hands. He waved for Travis to go next.

Travis stuck one leg through the window, then the other.

A tight cough came from behind them. "Halt. I'll shoot if I have to."

Electrified Ian pushed Travis, launched him out the window. "Go, Travis, go!" He whirled toward the man who'd threatened them. "What kind of a man are you that you'd shoot children?" He blocked the window with his body. "Jesus loves the little children..." He sang as loud as he could make his smoke-seared throat work. "All the children—" Coughing wracked his body. He bent, put his hands on his knees.

A pair of hands grabbed his belt from behind and jerked.

Ian banged his head and scraped his elbows on the window

frame, then was outside with bullets flying over his head. No one needed to tell him to crouch and run.

CHAPTER 33

THE SHOOTING STOPPED. Below the window, Williams slumped against the sanctuary wall and tried to catch his breath. "Adl—" He couldn't complete the word. He coughed so long and so hard he thought he'd pass out. But he didn't.

Thanks to Banks's incompetent decisions and orders, they'd had Hobart in custody for less than ten minutes. Thanks to the blessed smoke—Adler and the Major didn't die during the firefight.

He peered across the hazy, vacant room and stiffened. "Major?—Yardley?—Adler?"

His pulse thudded in the silence.

He rose and walked out of the sanctuary, through the foyer, and out the front doors.

In the moonlight, a light fog created enough glare he couldn't be certain. He strode down the pathway. The midnight-blue Studebaker Hawk he'd driven here stood in the parking lot— alone. "You were too cowardly to kill me yourselves?" he shouted.

A wave of nausea hit him. He bent, hands on knees and controlled his breathing. The nausea receded but his temples throbbed.

He tried to think back, figure out when they'd left.

Smoke had filled the whole sanctuary so blasted fast. He'd lunged for Hobart but the boy's kick landed on his shoulder. He couldn't hang on. Soon after that, the smoke overcame him. He choked and coughed and tears blinded him.

When the rebels had broken open the one window, it took precious minutes to clear enough to see Hobart at the window. Coughing threw off his aim.

Then he'd been stunned into a split-second of inaction when Hobart was yanked out the window. But it was enough. He missed his shot. And the rebels' barrage of gunfire ensured he didn't get another one.

The rebels' gunfire kept them pinned in that smoke-filled sanctuary for at least an hour.

Now Banks and Adler were gone. Nickerson, too. *So much for loyalty.*

He climbed into the car, too tired to stand. The Handie Talkie sat on the passenger seat. He shrugged. Might as well use it for personal purposes. He rubbed his eyes and face while he waited for the Handie Talkie to connect to the landlines.

"Hello?" the sound of his wife's voice made his chest hurt.

"Hello. It's me."

"You sound funny. Are you okay?"

"I love you and the children more than life itself."

A small gasp at the other end assured him that she'd recognized the signal.

"I love you." Her voice was strained. "Always."

After she hung up, he drank in the beauty of the moonlight and fog that shrouded the trees and turned the ruined old church into a mystical place.

"Banks—I didn't know you had it in you." He'd learned, too late, that superiors could be sneaky and underhanded like sleeper snitches.

He had no doubt that his superior would escape the judgment of the Azrael. What he didn't understand was why this had been the Lord's plan for him, but he knew judgment would come for Monty and Banks and the others—eventually.

On the drive back to the hotel, he thanked the Lord for the opportunity to experience life, for his loving wife, and his well-behaved children.

During the climb up to his fourth-floor room, he accepted his failure. He'd failed to acquire the Hobart children in the first place. He had failed this mission before Banks had arrived.

He squared his shoulders. It was his duty to give his life for the honor of the Cleaners.

Inside his hotel room, he shrugged off his jacket and dropped it on the bed. All he asked was that judgment wait until after he took a shower. He reached the bathroom door.

Click.

He turned and faced a dark shadowy form with the green eyes of night vision.

"We are Azrael."

A gun exploded.

A bright light flashed.

CHAPTER 34

IAN WOKE FIRST, his brother's heads pillowed on each side of his ribcage, his arms still wrapped around their shoulders. He had no idea how long he'd been sleeping but bright sunlight penetrated the tent walls and the smell of bacon made his stomach growl so loud that Travis stirred.

Travis bolted upright. He threw a glance around the tent, blew out a big breath, and bowed his head.

"It's okay, Trav. You're safe. We're all safe." Ian reached out and touched his hand.

Travis raised his head and beamed a big smile at him. "I knew you'd come for us."

Kenny rubbed his face and stretched. "I knew, too." He sat up and looked around. "Where's Leslie?"

"They took her straight to the place they're going to take us this morning."

Kenny tilted his head. "What place?"

A person's shadow fell across the tent flaps. "The place where you'll be safe and can grow up and be strong," Mrs. Underhill said.

Ian had seen her last night, but he still couldn't get over his surprise every time he saw proper Mrs. Underhill in a blouse and men's slacks. His history teacher as a rebel would take some getting used to.

"First, let's get you guys some breakfast."

"I smell bacon!" Travis and Kenny shouted and leaped up.

"Uh-uh," Ian said. "Roll your sleeping bags." The aromas of eggs and bacon and biscuits grew stronger, made his stomach ache and flooded his mouth with saliva.

Kenny and Travis worked together to smooth and flatten, fold, and roll the sleeping bags. They each had a left-over cough from the smoke, but laughed and shouted good-natured insults at one another, and scrambled out of the tent.

Ian stayed where he was for a moment, amazed that so many had risked their lives for him and his family. Mrs. Underhill and two men Ian had never met had provided the tent and watched over them while they slept.

He climbed out of the tent and found a mess of scrambled eggs and bacon and toast waiting for him on a smokeless camp stove.

While Ian and his brothers ate, the two men tore down and packed up camp. When they finished, one of the men cleaned up the dishes and stove. The other man used a branch from a fir tree to sweep the last signs of camp from the soil.

One of the strangers led the way. The boys each carried their own sleeping bag on their back, but two men that accompanied them carried the heavy rucksacks. Mrs. Underhill carried the A&P bag that bulged far more today than it had the last time Ian saw it.

"Who are we going to live with?" Kenny asked for the hundredth time. "Will Leslie be there?"

Mrs. Underhill smiled. "Yes. Your sister's already there. Our friends told us she's better this morning and waiting for you." She glanced over her shoulder at Ian. "Gertrude Howerton lives on the top of a mountain. She has a mule she calls Frank and she has chickens and goats and I don't know what else on her farm."

"Can I feed the goats?" Kenny asked.

Mrs. Underhill chuckled. "You'll have to ask her. Now Miss Gert—that's what you'll call her—can sound a little gruff sometimes. And she has a different way of greeting people. But don't let her scare you, she's really nice once you get to know her."

The boys trotted ahead, following the lead man.

Ian fell back to walk beside Mrs. Underhill who brought up the rear. "I don't need a place where I'll be safe and grow up and be strong. I want to join the rebels."

"We hoped you'd say that. But, your first job is to make sure your siblings are settled in."

"How long will that take?"

"That's up to them."

Ian scowled at the grass and considered turning around and going after Monty.

"Don't worry, Ian. You'll be busy while at Miss Gert's. She's a friend of ours. She'll help you train."

"Train me? You have to train to be a rebel?"

"Some. But we have plans for you, Ian. From time-to-time, myself or Mr. Collins will visit. One of those times, we'll have an assignment for you."

Ian raised his gaze. Beyond the trees ahead, sunlight poured into a meadow. No, it wasn't a meadow. He drew up even with his brothers still uncertain what it was.

"What is this place?" Travis asked.

"This is Miss Gert's home."

Ian left the trees and stepped into a small glade filled to overflowing. Clusters of boxes and a variety of discarded furniture formed a labyrinth. Its walls were three feet wide and shoulder high. Jagged bits and pieces of broken glass, barbed wire, and sharpened stakes jutted out of the top of the walls.

"It looks like a dum—"

Ian clamped a hand on Kenny's shoulder. "Be nice." But he had to agree, it looked like a dump.

Inside the labyrinth sat a lopsided house patched with tarpaper and blue tarps. The outbuildings looked safer to Ian than the house did.

A scrawny old woman with long gray braids stood in front of the entrance to the labyrinth. She wore a baggy, orange and green plaid shirt and red and black checkered pants and—

Ian's mouth fell open—she held a red fireman's axe. The same axe she'd carried on the mule at the farm where he'd stolen the eggs.

About sixty feet from the old woman, Mrs. Underhill said, "Stop." She froze in place. "No one move. Miss Gert has her way of checking people out. I promise, she won't hurt you, but let her do her thing. Then we can go inside. Remember, *don't move.*"

Kenny and Travis and Ian stood rock still.

The old woman shouldered her axe and sniffed the wind, stepped closer and closer, and sniffed the wind again. She cocked her head one way, then the other. "Lawd, ye said the boys was children. These two is half-grown men." She poked the head of her axe into Ian's stomach.

Ian gasped at the gentle touch, more surprised than hurt. He didn't move but shot a glance at Mrs. Underhill.

She gave him a slight nod. "They've conducted themselves like full-grown men, but have a ways to go before they're of legal age."

The old woman cocked her head again, regarded the three boys for a long moment. Chickens squawked and goats bleated in the background. "M'name's Gertrude Howerton. You will call me Miss Gert." She lowered the axe and let it hang at her side. "Reckon y'all are tuckered out and need to sit a-spell. Follow me."

She led them into the maze. "You mustn't try to get back

through this here lab-ee-rinth without me until ye been trained."
She paused, cleared a snare, waved them through. "Take ten
steps and stop." She reset the snare and wriggled past them to
lead again. She stopped for four more traps, traps Ian didn't
recognize.

She led them into the inner courtyard. Chickens wandered
freely, pecking at the grassy courtyard.

From here, Ian could see the mule and a bunch of goats
grazing in a corral. Mrs. Underhill touched his shoulder and
pointed toward the house.

Miss Gert climbed the rickety front porch steps. At the
threshold, she hesitated and muttered something under her
breath. She turned around three times and without pause or
explanation, entered her home.

Kenny giggled, ran up the steps, and stopped. He muttered
gibberish and turned around three times, then entered the house.
"Leslie!"

Travis shrugged and followed Kenny without turning circles.

Ian grabbed Mrs. Underhill's arm, held her back. "I need to
know a little more about this Miss Gert."

Mrs. Underhill put an arm around Ian's shoulders. "You've
handled Second Sphere agents pretty darn well. I don't think
you'll have any trouble with Miss Gert."

"Ian, come quick!" Travis called from inside the doorway.

Ian dashed up the rickety porch steps. It took a couple of
moments for his eyes to adjust to the dark interior. To his right,
stood the kitchen. Travis stood behind a battered chrome and
Formica table piled high with bottles of every shape, size, and
color. Behind Travis were stacks of boxes and crates filled with
empty bottles.

Travis's eyes twinkled and a grin stretched across his face.
"Leslie's awake. She wants to see you."

"Awake?" *That must mean she's better.* He followed Travis down a narrow aisle defined by walls of boxes and crates.

They passed a cramped space with a lumpy sofa and wooden rocker facing a large, stone fireplace. Down the aisle, on the other side of the room, sat a bed with a scrolled wrought iron headboard pushed up against a window draped with faded curtains. In the middle of the bed, sat Kenny nestled next to Leslie.

She looked up when Ian entered the room. "You did it."

Warmth spread through Ian's chest. He hurried to the side of the bed, took her hand. It was dry and calloused and warm. "How do you feel?"

"Like I slid down a mountain and broke my leg but I'll live—thanks to you and the doctor." She lifted shining eyes to O'Brien who stood back in a dark corner.

Ian tried to think of some way to say more than thank you.

O'Brien dipped his head, picked up his bag, and followed Mrs. Underhill. They disappeared into the aisle of boxes and crates.

"Wait 'til you see our bedroom," Travis said. He'd taken a seat on an upside down crate next to the bed.

"We get to climb a ladder up to our beds," Kenny said. "And Miss Gert says I can help her feed the goats. I hope they like me."

"You've turned into part mountain goat yourself, " Ian said. "They'll like you." He glanced from Kenny to Travis and back to Leslie.

They were alone, but no longer alone and they had a new life to live.

CHAPTER 35

A Testament for Modern Times
  The New Book of Josiah
  Chapter 50, verses 103-110

> 106. *Woe be unto the unrepentant sinner. Thy name has been removed from the Book of Life.*
> 107. *Behold a host of angels, the Azrael, stand between the earth and the heaven.*
> 108. *And the angels will bless and pass over those who wield the shield of the Fellowship.*
> 109. *But Azrael shall ceaselessly scour the land for the wicked.*
> 110. *For she shall execute judgement in His name.*

THANK YOU

for dedicating some of you time to reading my story. I want to write books readers love to read. So please, leave an honest review on the site where you bought this book or Goodreads or my website. Your review doesn't have to be long or literary. A simple I loved it or hated it and a star rating will do.

All reviews are gratefully received.

———

THE STORY DOESN'T END HERE

THANK YOU

Thank you for dedicating a chunk of your valuable time to read this story. I want to write books readers love to read. So please, leave an honest review on the site where you bought this book or on a review site like Goodreads. Your review doesn't have to be long or literary. Please mention that you received the book for free without obligation then, simple I loved it or hated it and a star rating will do.

All reviews are gratefully received.

THE STORY DOESN'T END HERE

Keep reading for the opening chapters of Book One of the Fellowship Dystopia, ***My Soul to Keep***. See more of Gert and a glimpse of Ian and Leslie. Follow Miranda and Beryl's adventures set in this same dystopian world.

Available at all your favorite online bookstores.

EXCERPT FROM MY SOUL TO KEEP

BOOK ONE OF THE FELLOWSHIP DYSTOPIA SERIES

THE GIANT BRONZE angel of death loomed over Miranda Clarke's shoulder. The statue, *Shield of Mercy, Hand of Justice*, stood at the grand entrance of the Fellowship Center as it had for all of Miranda's life. With Uncle Sam sheltered in her great black wings, the angel hovered over the fallen body of President-elect Franklin Delano Roosevelt and pointed to the pile of ash where the assassin had stood. Was it the statue or was it the tiny flare of rebellion inside her that made Miranda hesitate?

Tom, her bodyguard, closed the space between them, stood too close. "Is something wrong?"

Nothing. And everything. She hid her fears behind an angelic daughter-of-the-councilor smile. "I need to powder my nose."

"They'll be seating your family in five minutes. Tell me what you need, I'll have someone fetch it."

I need to not be the councilor's daughter. Gazing across the foyer, Miranda's pulse cranked up a notch.

Hundreds of men in sharkskin suits and women in taffeta dresses filled the foyer, waiting for the auditorium doors to open. Clusters of them here and there held onto their hats, an assortment of felt, feathers, netting, and ruffles, and peered up at the mural-painted dome five stories above. They reeked of aftershave lotions, cheap colognes, and forbidden cigarette smoke.

"There are some things a girl must do on her own." Miranda dove into a sea of elbows and padded shoulders, big purses, and voluminous skirts. Her bodyguard followed.

Miranda avoided the knot of people clustered around Senator Joseph P. Kennedy, Jr. People who noticed her moved out of her way. She wished they wouldn't notice. She longed for a regular life, a job, and her own apartment. It was 1961, for goodness' sake. You'd think it would be acceptable for a girl to be on her own. But Mama said the Fellowship rules were there for a reason. Mama had survived the horrors of the Great Depression. She'd often spoken of how suicides and murders during that time made the waters of the Potomac outside run red. Mama said that the Fellowship had saved the country. And that top Fellowship members had a duty to be consummate examples and ambassadors. But Miranda didn't want to be an exemplary Fellowship member. She didn't want an arranged marriage. And she didn't want all the public duties and appearances. She wanted to help people, not ask them to donate to the charity of the hour. Somehow she had to convince her parents she should be a guardian. She could be a good example, serving the poor and underprivileged—in private.

A pimple-faced young man materialized before her.

"Sister Clarke, what an honor." His soft, plump hand gripped hers and pumped their hands up and down with youthful exuberance.

"My pleasure." She tried to extract her hand.

He reinforced his grip with his other hand.

She took in a sharp breath. He couldn't be one of Mama's "potential matches." Mama had said she'd talk to Daddy about Miranda's guardianship training.

"Say cheese."

Miranda turned toward the voice.

A flashbulb popped.

Black dots swam in her vision.

An arm pushed into the space between her and Pimple-Face and broke the young man's grip. Tom stiff-armed her behind his back and pushed Pimple-Face away. He jerked the camera out of the photographer's hands, flipped the back of the camera open, and shoved it back into the photographer's chest.

The photographer grabbed his camera, and Tom yanked out the film.

"You can't do that." The photographer glared at Tom.

Tom folded his arms across his chest and quirked an eyebrow at the young man.

The photographer's gaze wavered. He swallowed hard and exchanged looks with Pimple-Face. They backed away into the crowd.

Miranda glanced around. The curious and judgmental circled them like the Romans had surrounded the Christians in the arena. *Probably giving me a thumbs-down too.* "It's nothing. A misunderstanding." Her daughter-of-the-councilor voice sounded reassuring, at least on the outside.

Amid murmurs and shuffling feet, the people around them returned to interrupted conversations.

Tom seized her elbow and guided her to the nearest wall.

"I'm fine, Tom." Her words sounded sharper than she'd intended.

He had been her bodyguard since she was a little girl. From his crew cut to his expensive tailored suit, and his ever-on-alert attitude, he was unmistakable and inescapable.

She tugged against his grip. "All he wanted was a picture."

Something dark and predatory flashed across Tom's face. "You don't know what he wanted."

"Neither do you." Miranda pried his fingers from her elbow

and stalked away, ignoring the urge to scrub his touch off. She'd tried to tell Mama that Tom took small liberties. Mama had frowned and said, "Pray that the words of a harlot be scoured from your mind and tongue."

Miranda hurried through the pink marble colonnade supporting the balconies above and slipped through a door, relieved for the chance to be rid of him, even if just for a moment.

Accustomed to long waits outside the ladies' room, Tom planted himself outside the door.

Inside, women and children jammed the space, jostled for empty stalls and sinks. Voices, clattering heels, and the whoosh of flushing echoed off the granite walls.

Miranda pulled off her gloves, tucked them into her pocket, and waited for an empty stall.

"You're late, Miranda." Her sister's loud alto rose across the room.

Irene stood at the end of the counter. She peered into the mirror and stabbed a hatpin into her tiny, platter-shaped hat. The hat matched her mint green dress and complemented her copper-colored hair.

"Don't wait for me." Miranda waved Irene away. But Irene always waited. It was as if she were Miranda's personal do-right angel.

"Hurry. Mama will be annoyed if we enter after the lights go down."

The next stall opened up.

Miranda locked the door and braced her hands and forehead against the cool metal. She couldn't bear one more family procession to their front row seats. *Maybe, if I wait long enough, Irene will leave without me.* A long time ago, she would fantasize about escaping out of the window above the fainting couch. *But fantasy isn't reality.* Miranda sighed. Life as a guardian wouldn't be easy, but it would be out of the public eye.

She waited and listened. The noisy voices of excited women and children grew less and less.

"Miranda? What's taking so long?"

"I'm constipated." It sounded more like a question than a statement.

"Then it won't hurt to hold it a few more hours."

Miranda bowed her head and her shoulders sagged. *One more time won't kill me.* She flushed the toilet and exited the stall with her head high and shoulders squared.

Irene stood with her back against the mirror, her arms crossed, and an impatient frown.

Miranda crossed to the sink and washed her hands.

The ladies' room attendant handed her a towel.

Miranda dried her hands and dropped the towel into the attendant's waiting hand. She stole a glance at her younger sister's reflection.

Two years Miranda's junior, Irene had a plump matron's demeanor and confidence. She had embraced marriage and motherhood, making her a success in their mother's eyes. By comparison, Miranda was an about-to-be-an-undesirable, twenty-five-year-old spinster. Miranda becoming a guardian would allow Mama to save face.

"We're going to the beach house this weekend," Irene said. "You should come too."

"I have other plans." Miranda fluffed her bangs, shielding her face, hiding the lie.

"Plans can change." Irene sounded pleased with herself. "That baby blue dotted Swiss is lovely on you."

"Thank you." Miranda smoothed the nubby fabric of her skirt and studied Irene through her lashes, suspicious of the compliment. Mama had insisted Miranda wear her best dress.

"We mustn't be late." Irene latched onto Miranda's wrist, dragged her out of the bathroom and into the hall. There, Irene's husband and four-year-old daughter waited, as did their bodyguards.

Irene snapped her fingers at Felix. "Fix Sandra's collar." She swept past them, pulling Miranda toward the auditorium.

Miranda cast a sympathetic glance at her brother-in-law.

Felix had a receding hairline, big ears, and an I'm-drowning-in-love expression fixed on Irene. He looked dumber than he was. He smoothed Sandra's collar and fell in behind Irene, towing their daughter behind him.

Their bodyguards trailed after.

Hunched over like a fat gargoyle, the director of the Fellowship Center sat on a stool by the auditorium door. "Mr. and Mrs. Earnshaw. Miss Clarke." He rocked the stool in his rush to greet them. "The Fellowship Center welcomes you, our honored guests. May I escort you to your seats?" He threw the auditorium doors open in a make-room, make-room way, took Irene's arm, and strutted down the aisle.

Felix picked up Sandra and hurried to follow.

Miranda stopped in the doorway, turned back toward the ladies' room.

Her bodyguard stepped in, cutting her off.

"I need to powder my nose."

"You just did."

She glanced around with pretended furtiveness and then whispered, "It's my time of the month."

Tom scoffed. "That was last week. If you're having problems, you need to talk to your mother." He gestured toward the door.

She raised her chin and walked into the auditorium.

Irene, Felix, and Sandra reached the first row before her. They slipped past Uncle Weldon and Mama and sat at the far end, next to David, Miranda's younger brother.

Miranda held her skirt close and squeezed past Uncle Weldon, who sat in the aisle seat. Weldon, Mama's younger brother, had the same hawkish nose as Mama and had deep-set eyes and a thin upper lip that drooped downward in a forever frown.

Next to him sat Mama. Small and thin, Mama was made of sharp angles.

Miranda had no choice but to take the last seat available, the one next to Mama.

Mama rested her cool, dry hand on Miranda's, a holdover from her childhood. The pressure of Mama's hand had increased whenever a child squirmed or whispered.

At seven o'clock sharp, the crimson velvet curtains rose. In center stage sat a raised podium that bore the symbol of the Fellowship: a blood-red shield sectioned by a white cross.

The audience shushed and settled in their seats.

A moment later Miranda's father, Councilor Donald Clarke, strode onto the stage, his burgundy robes sweeping the floor behind him. He took his place at the podium.

At home, he was grumpy and gloomy. On stage, he transformed into a super-charged beacon of love for his fellow man. The spotlight lightened his swarthy skin, made his dark pompadour gleam, and added angles to the softness of his long face.

Daddy read from the First Book of Josiah in a quiet, conversational voice. "It came to pass after the Great War, the days of darkness, the Great Depression, fell upon us..."

His rich baritone and soft Southern accent rose without strain. "Thugs, thieves, and murderers ruled our land.

"After the assassination of President-elect Roosevelt, Prophet Josiah gathered the Fellowship and prayed for deliverance. And the Lord sent the Angels of Death, the Azrael, to cleanse the wicked from our land.

"The people's prayers were answered. The thugs and thieves and murderers were scoured from our lives. And America was saved from the strife across the sea. Out of the ashes of the old, divided world of Great Britain and Europe and the Third Reich, the United Federation of Germany arose. Peace and prosperity returned."

Miranda tuned out the sermon and imagined what her life as a guardian would be. A life free from public scrutiny and criticism. No more charity and political dinners. Sadly, she would also give up cruising the bay, skeet shooting, and island picnics. But she deserved—no, she needed—the quiet guardian's life.

"—Miranda."

She started. *Why did Daddy say my name?* Everyone was staring at her. Mama wore her public smile, but her eyes shot fierce, unspoken commands at Miranda.

Mama nudged her foot.

"Miranda? Won't you come up on stage?"

Her stomach plunged like an anchor. *He knows I hate getting up in front of people.*

Mama gripped Miranda's arm in a shark-bite grasp and stood, pulling Miranda to her feet.

Her legs quivered, boneless. She teetered. Her mother's grip tightened, kept her upright.

Miranda arranged her face into her daughter-of-the-councilor mask and willed strength to her legs.

Mama steered her onto the stage.

"Ladies and gentlemen, my wife and I are pleased to include you in a special surprise for my beautiful daughter." He escorted her to center stage. "Wait right here. Your mother and I will be over there." He positioned her facing stage left, then he and Mama faded into the shadows.

The stage lights dimmed, leaving Miranda centered in a cone of light. The bright light blinded her. Blinded to the audience. Blinded to her parents. Blinded to what was coming.

Murmurs and rustlings came from the audience. Soft chords

of "Moonlight Serenade" rose from the piano. Her stomach pretzeled. *This isn't how one announces a novice guardian.*

Ryan Mitchell stepped into the light. He had wavy blond hair, green eyes, and a cleft in his chin. His dark blue suit with its wide lapels broadened his shoulders.

Her thoughts scrambled. *What is he doing here?*

Her parents had bought the beach house in Nassawadox when she was six years old. She and Ryan had been summertime neighbors and dueling sandcastle architects ever since. He'd gotten sweet on her. Something she'd politely discouraged.

"Hello." The dimple in his left cheek appeared and disappeared like it always did when he was nervous.

"Hello." *I have to get off this stage.*

He put one hand in and out of his pocket, straightened his tie, and smoothed his lapel.

Back the way I came or backstage?

"Remember when we first met?"

"Yes."

"You were six, playing on the beach. I thought, why did a stupid girl have to move next door?" He gazed at her with I'm-in-love-eyes and reached into his pocket.

Her councilor's-daughter mask and councilor's-daughter smile vanished. Her heart stuttered. She'd told him friends, *only* friends.

"By the end of the summer, we were building sandcastles together. By the time you were sixteen, I knew." He knelt on one knee.

The audience gasped.

Her lungs quit. Her heart skipped a beat. She spun and darted toward backstage, breaking every councilor's-daughter rule in existence.

She didn't know where she was going. Didn't care.

CHAPTER 2

MIRANDA RAN behind the curtains into the dark right wing. Hands clamped down on her shoulders, brought her to a solid stop. She twisted to see Tom, her bodyguard.

"Let me go." A wooden rack on the wall held dozens of ropes that stretched like strings on a giant harp to curtains and equipment overhead. *No door. No ladder.*

Miranda's blood pounded *run-run-run* through her brain. *To the left? Yes.* An Exit sign glowed red above a door.

"Please. I've got to get out of here." She wriggled, but couldn't break Tom's grip.

"You know I can't let you go."

"You're supposed to protect me." Her words rasped through her throat.

"Protect you? From what? A proposal?"

"From losing—" Words could not express the wrongness. —*who I am.*

He cocked his head and stared down at her like she was a twit, a lunatic.

She wasn't crazy. Accepting Ryan's proposal meant a lifetime of political and charity dinners and... No, she couldn't do it. Not now. Not ever. Miranda forced herself to relax.

Tom's hold loosened.

She lunged, freed herself, and ran.

He grabbed her arm. *Riiiiip.* He spun her around and pulled her close—full body contact close.

She raised her gaze from his Adam's apple to his face.

His eyes traveled down to her chest, his expression less and less bodyguard and more and more brute.

A chill rippled across her skin. Miranda glanced down. The right side of her bodice had ripped and folded over revealing her V-neck, lace slip. Her face flamed. She reached for the torn fabric, but his grip tightened to bone bruising. Her chest constricted. She drew quick, shallow breaths. Her vision blurred.

Footsteps approached.

He forced her backward, leaving a decency space between them.

His hungry stare at her cleavage made her want to shrivel to nothing. She lowered her head. Her tears dripped onto the floor.

The hem of Mama's royal blue dress and matching pumps appeared beside Tom's size elevens.

"Young lady, are you trying to ruin your father and me?" Mama's cool, dry fingers lifted Miranda's chin.

"I can't marry Ryan. I—" Miranda swallowed her vow that she didn't love Ryan. "I'm going to be a guardian."

"Release her," Mama said. Her command was low and brusque.

Tom released Miranda so fast she had to take a half step to keep from falling.

Mama jerked her chin toward the stage door.

Tom crossed the space. Facing them, he'd replaced his leer with an impersonal stare. He spread his feet and crossed his arms over his chest, making himself an impenetrable wall between Miranda and escape.

"What have you done to yourself?" Irritation colored Mama's whisper.

Miranda focused on her dress. Her waistline sash was off center, her bodice twisted and bunched, the nubby fabric torn and frayed. She straightened her bodice and held the loose part to her chest.

"Stop slouching." Mama scrubbed Miranda's tears away with a starched, lace handkerchief. "The idea that you have to love someone *before* you marry him is storybook nonsense." Mama folded and put away her handkerchief. "I did not love your father when we got married. We were an ordained match, like you and Ryan. We grew to love one another—over time." Mama's voice softened, offered kindness. "I was as frightened the day we married as you are today."

"I'm not you, Mama."

"*You* were born with privileges *I* never had. Believe me, you do not want the dark days to return. Famine, murder, pestilence, and disease—we lived in fear. Be grateful you don't." Mama glanced over Miranda's shoulder toward the stage.

Hesitantly Miranda looked. The choir and audience sang a happy hymn. Ryan had moved out of the spotlight, into the shadows, staring at something in his hand.

"Look at me." Mama grabbed Miranda's wrists.

Miranda whipped her head around, faced her mother.

"It's a good match." Mama wetted her lips. "Ryan is one of us, one of the Elect. He has a future. He'll be a senator or councilor one day. And you *like* him. What more do you want?" Mama's voice and grip tightened with each whispered word.

She will never understand. "I'll make a good guardian, I promise."

Mama exhaled an impatient "pfft." "You are the daughter of the future First Apostle." Mama grabbed Miranda's chin, locked a shriveling glare on her. "You will *not* invite the wrath of Azrael.

You *will* marry Ryan. You will be happy. And, someday, you will fall in love."

"What if I never love Ryan?" Miranda's chin trembled.

Mama brushed Miranda's cheek with hers, made a kiss-kiss sound. "Go apologize. Accept Ryan's proposal. Poor boy thinks he's been rejected."

Miranda threw a desperate glance behind her. She'd have to run onto the stage, past the choir, past Daddy and Ryan, up the aisle and out of the auditorium, and across the foyer to the doors. No way she'd make it. She faced Mama again.

"You can't go on stage like that." Mama yanked out one of her hatpins and jabbed it at Miranda.

Miranda stepped back.

"I'm not going to stab you," Mama whispered fiercely. "Let me fix this." She knocked Miranda's hand away, folded the ripped edges together, and wove the pin through the fabric. Mama used a second hatpin to secure the side seam. She stepped back, surveyed Miranda head-to-toe. "Smile."

Miranda dredged up a mask with a dutiful daughter's smile, a mask she feared would not hold.

Mama twirled Miranda around. "Make it a good show." Mama shoved her.

Miranda stumbled onto the stage.

The audience gasped.

Ryan jerked his head around, rushed toward her, then froze, pinned in the spotlight.

The pianist and choir stopped in mid-chorus.

It was as if a monster had stepped onto the stage. A monster named Miranda.

Miranda could barely stand, barely breathe, barely hang onto her sanity. Her hands clenched and unclenched in a battle between the monster and the good daughter.

Mama appeared on her left, Tom on her right. They crowded her, nudging and pushing her forward.

A moment before they reached center stage, Mama swept past Miranda and took her place beside Daddy. Tom faded into the shadows.

Miranda took a shaky breath and forced her feet to move. She stepped into the spotlight.

Two bright spots on Ryan's cheeks shone in his pale face. His dimple had vanished.

Miranda opened her mouth to make the expected apology. Words congealed in her throat. No sound came out. She closed her mouth and clamped her teeth on her tongue.

Mama cleared her throat.

Miranda glanced at her parents.

Daddy waited with the expression of a long-suffering saint. Mama had her councilor's-wife smile on her lips but her eyes held a you-dare-not-cross-me threat.

A coppery taste flooded Miranda's mouth. She faced Ryan again. "I'm told that most brides get cold feet." She gave a half-hearted shrug. "I guess I get cold, *running* feet."

Ryan threw back his head and laughed a too-hearty laugh.

The audience roared as if she'd uttered the funniest thing they'd ever heard.

She nodded to the pianist. *Let's get this over with.*

"Moonlight Serenade" drifted across the stage.

Miranda offered Ryan her left hand.

He squeezed her fingers tight. His warm hands did not warm her icy one. She wished the floor would swallow her, or that lightning would strike her, or even that an Azrael would Take her. But no rescue came.

Ryan knelt. He pulled a ring out of his pocket and offered the diamond to her. "Will you marry me?" His dimple winked in his cheek. Then he whispered, "And promise to always keep me smiling?"

Her chest was hollow, empty, an eternal pit of despair.

"Yes." *Too sharp.* She softened her voice. "I will."

He slid the ring on her finger.

Miranda's vision narrowed, focused on the much-larger-than-a-carat, round solitaire. The ring was so far away she could almost imagine it was on someone else's hand. As a little girl, she'd dreamed of a fairytale romance and proposal. She'd never guessed that fairy tales could warp into nightmares.

Mama made a soft noise.

Miranda forced a bright-for-the-audience-smile. She raised her hand for the crowd. The diamond winked in the spotlight.

The audience burst into applause.

"Cold running feet." Daddy barked a stage laugh. "That's my funny girl. Come on, boy. Kiss her. It's okay. You're engaged."

Ryan stood, wrapped her in a tender embrace, and kissed her deeply.

Miranda felt as if she were drowning in a pool full of wet cement.

CHAPTER 3

ANNA CLIMBED through a jagged area where the barn wall had rotted. The still, musty air tickled her nose. She clamped her lips tight and held in her sneeze, making her ears pop. Uncle said operational silence was more important than momentary discomfort. She scouted the barn, like Uncle had taught her. Six empty stalls ran down one side, and near the locked barn doors stood a gleaming green tractor. Attached to the tractor were rows of shiny discs for turning the soil. A workbench loaded with tools lined the opposite wall. At the end of the workbench, a ladder led to the loft.

The loft was perfect. There were bundles of hay and lots of old junk to hide behind. A faint breeze came through the open loft door and holes in the roof. The air smelled sweet, scented with hay and growing things.

She crept to the loft door and peeked out. Papa Locke, Aunt Allyson, Uncle, and his lady-friend gathered in a knot on the hillside, talking. They couldn't see her 'cause she stayed back in the shadow. Uncle had told her that she was the very best hider. Anna believed it. Every now and then, she'd see "It" catch one of the other players trying to find a hiding place or trying to tag home. She wasn't going to try to tag home. It would catch her, like all the others. She would wait for the "olly olly oxen free," and she'd win 'cause no one could find her.

Anna liked living on the farm. The math classes and science classes were hard, but half the day they played games: bullet-bullet, who's got the bullet; conceal-and-stalk; and capture-the-unbeliever. It was fun.

Tired of being still, she explored the loft. Hay bales were stacked around an old school desk where mice had once nested, a pile of old tractor tires, and a rusted bicycle. A mewling sound drew her around another stack of hay. The sound came from seven tiny kittens in a nest of hay. They nuzzled hungrily against one another, making little crying noises.

"Are you special-born, like me?" She gathered them into her lap. One climbed her overalls. Another suckled on one of the overall buttons. A scrabbling sound beneath her made her remember the game. She swiped the kittens off her lap and threw herself flat against the hay. The noise grew closer. A cat sprang onto the loft floor. The cat scrambled over the hay and checked out her kittens. Soon, the cat settled down and nursed her babies.

After each kitten drank its fill, it curled into a ball and slept. When the last one had finished, the mother cat washed herself and her sleeping kittens with her tongue.

"What a nice mommy you are." Anna held her hand out for the cat to sniff. "You came back to feed your babies." She picked up the cat and put it in her lap. The animal stiffened, hair raised on its back. Anna petted it, crooned to it. "Nice kitty." The fur was smooth and soft and warm. The cat lay down in Anna's lap and purred.

Anna reclined against the hay bale behind her and stroked the cat. She wished It would give up. A faint sound grew louder, more recognizable. Voices. Papa Locke, Aunt Allyson, Uncle, and his lady-friend too. They stopped underneath the loft door. Anna stayed still and hoped they wouldn't come into the barn.

"Reproduction happens when a sperm and an egg combine to create a zygote. In parthenogenesis there is no sperm, there is no meiosis; therefore, the offspring is haploid." Papa Locke always talked that way 'cause he was an important scientist doctor.

"Parth-en-o-gen-sis? Doc, you gotta come up with a better sales pitch."

Anna stifled her giggle behind her hand. Uncle sounded silly when he tried to talk like Papa Locke.

"We trick the egg into acting like there is sperm," Aunt Allyson explained. She was Teacher.

"Once we have a successful parthenote—"

"Doc, our customers need simple, one-syllable words."

"Partheno from the Greek for virgin birth." Aunt Allyson was a good teacher.

"'Virgin birth' is sacrilegious," argued Uncle's lady-friend. She always argued. "Couldn't we call it cloning?"

Papa made his irritated-at-you sound in his throat. "It's not cloning. There is no transfer of a nucleus from a donor cell to an enucleated oocyte. Rather, the oocyte is stimulated to divide." Papa and the others moved away from the barn.

Anna was glad. Adults never were as interesting as they thought they were. She stroked the momma cat sleeping in her lap and closed her eyes.

"Anna?"

She started upright. The mother cat's claws pierced Anna's overalls and raked her skin. "Ow!" She grabbed the cat around its belly.

The cat clawed wildly, scratched her arm, drew blood.

"Bad cat." Anna threw the cat as hard as she could. It soared up into the air, over the edge of the loft.

The cat corkscrewed in mid-air, twisted her front, then her back, and pointed all four feet toward the floor. She dropped. Slammed into the sharp discs below.

A piercing yowl of pain split the air.

Then silence.

Anna's nostrils flared, taking in the coppery odor of death. A lighter-than-air sensation filled her chest and made her skin tingle. For an instant, she hovered above everything. The lightness vanished, and she ached with the absence of her power.

"Anna?" A head, then Aunt Allyson's frowning face appeared at the top of the loft ladder. She glanced around. "What happened?"

"It was a bad cat." Anna glanced at the dead cat, then Aunt Allyson. "It left her babies when they were hungry. And it hurt us." Anna held out her arm for inspection. "We had to punish it."

"'And she shall execute judgment in righteousness,'" Aunt Allyson said. She stood, stepped away from the loft's edge, and inspected Anna's arm. "Let no man nor beast raise his hand to hurt you."

One of the kittens opened its eyes and mewed. Anna picked it up. "You asked and are granted life." She looked at the other orphans nested together, sleeping. "Thy will be done."

———

My Soul to Keep is available at most online book retailers.

AFTERWORD

A Note to Readers

Why would I write about a dark world that I would not want to live in?

I moved seventeen times before I graduated from high school. No, I was not a military brat. When asked why, my parents said the frequent moves were to find better jobs, better houses, a better life.

It was difficult to make friendships when you figured you wouldn't stay long. So, the characters I read about in books became my best friends, my confidants, and my heroes whose examples inspired me. It's no wonder I became a writer.

My first published story was a children's story. It appeared in a now-defunct regional magazine for children called **Wee Wisdom**. I had two other children's stories published in regional and national publications.

A story written in collaboration with Rob Chilson was my first science fiction sale. **The White Box** appeared in Analog Science Fiction Science Fact magazine. A second **Box** story also appeared in **Analog.** They were much, much longer than my children's stories. I discovered I liked longer stories. It gave me more opportunity to write characters with depth and challenges.

I write about people, events, and locations that inspire my books, progress updates and sneak peeks on my blog. Read all about it. Sign Me Up.

Book two of the Fellowship Dystopia series, *If I Should Die*, will be available online in early 2022.

ACKNOWLEDGMENTS

While writing is a solitary occupation, it also requires help from many people. I am grateful for the help of these amazing friends, mentors, beta readers, and editors:

Rob Chilson

Dora Furlong

Jan S. Gephardt

Julie Glover

Terry Matz

Lisa Norman

Alison Tellure

Sidekick Jenn

William F. Wu

And the Writers-in-Rob's-Living-Room.

FINALLY, I wouldn't be writing at all without the unfailing support and love of my husband and number one fan. I miss you.